GHOST OF A CHANCE

GHOST OF A CHANCE

PROVIDENCE PARANORMAL COLLEGE BOOK EIGHT

D.R. PERRY

LMBPN

DISRUPTIVE IMAGINATION

Copyright © 2016 D.R. Perry
Cover by Fantasy Book Design
Cover copyright © LMBPN Publishing

LMBPN Publishing
PMB 196, 2540 South Maryland Pkwy
Las Vegas, NV 89109

Version 2.1 November 2022
ebook ISBN: 978-1-64971-885-3
Print ISBN: 978-1-64971-886-0

CHAPTER ONE

Horace

I floated high in the air above Bianca Brighton as she checked for ghost issues on the first day of classes at good old Providence Paranormal College. I gazed down at her newly lavender hair, distracted. She'd dyed it just about every color of the rainbow at some point. I wasn't sure why she'd changed it to that delicate shade of purple, though she usually told me just about everything. Ghosts and their Mediums often became best friends. Once they'd bonded by sharing a body with possession, however, the partnership got permanent. But we hadn't crossed that line yet. I was too chicken for that.

The lecture hall had such great acoustics I wondered why that vampire punk band didn't play in here instead of the Nocturnal Lounge. I couldn't figure out a thing about the undead, especially since they didn't tend to leave ghosts, and I hadn't met many while I was still solid. Dragons were a different matter altogether. Almost every single one of them that died left ghosts. Exceptionally disgruntled ones, too. And Blaine Harcourt's two dead dads were more annoying than most.

"All I'm saying is, you shouldn't have been so hard on my boy, Wilfred." I didn't bother looking over my shoulder at the ghost of Ignacius Harcourt. I knew his square, handsome features would be cast in a mold of barely concealed anger, ironically framed by his shaggy, auburn hair. That hair and his temper were two of the legacies he'd left Blaine.

"And I say your kid needed more tough love than even I could dish out." Wilfred snorted. "He was lucky to have me. Just look at the situation his mother has put him in now and tell me again how he should have had it easier, Iggy."

"Don't you dare call me that, or so help me—"

"Knock it off." This time, I turned fully around, using both hands to snap my fingers in front of their two faces at the same time. "Just look at what all your bickering is doing and shut your traps already." I flattened my hand and gestured at the chaos below.

The ghosts of dragons past went silent as they watched what looked like an entire ream of paper scattering around the room below us. Some of the last airborne pieces see-sawed their way down courtesy of gravity we ghosts didn't have to obey. Each sheet bore the bolded header "Fall Syllabus," and some were pursued by dismayed students.

"I'm sorry," said Wilfred. I nodded, then glared at his longer-dead verbal sparring partner.

"Yes, I realize I should know better." Ignacius rolled his eyes, looking exactly like his son, Blaine. "I ought to just hide away somewhere, even if it means losing all my marbles and going wraith."

"You know better, Ig." The oldest ghost I knew leaned against nothing, tilting the tricorn hat he always wore askew on his white-wigged head. "And if Mister Horace Lancaster here didn't try to stop you, you'd both risk losing your jobs with the College. Because I'd have to go through channels to tell the Headmistress about your bad behavior."

"I don't like tattle-tails, Rob." I put one fist against my hip and brandished the other. "No one does."

"Actually, everyone solid does, especially the ones who aren't able to see us," Rob smirked. "This is an Incorporeal Studies course, and I've got more experience with teaching this sort of thing than you, Porous Horace."

"Just in case time has addled what passes for your brain, sir, we're all porous." Wilfred's sick burn reminded me that the dragon ghost still had some figurative teeth.

"Quit sucking up to me." I almost felt guilty for pointing at the still-scattered syllabi and glaring again. "If you really want points with Skeleton Crew management, go and help those poor kids clean your mess up, already."

"You know you're a huge square, Horace, right?" Rob's eyes twinkled with a child-like glee, then crinkled at the corners. Typical behavior from him.

"At least I'm a shape other than round." I side-eyed Rob's portly figure.

"What can I say? I felt like being plump today." His hat changed color from black to red, an ectoplasmic testament to his ghostly willpower and long experience. Of course, he'd use it on something frivolous and cosmetic like that. The fact that he hung around with the youngest confirmed medium in Providence made complete sense, considering his immature jokes. "Uncool. Is that the reason you and Miss Bianca haven't sealed your deal yet?"

"Knock it off, Rob. I mean, seriously." I shook my head, adjusting the bowler hat I favored. "We shouldn't be making each other angry. It's bad enough with double dragon trouble all the time over here." I sighed, shaking my head as Wilfred and Ignacius continued their dead dad rivalry while gathering syllabi into a pile that resembled a bird's nest.

"I think your medium might need some extra help this semester." Rob winked.

"What's that supposed to mean?" I jerked my chin at Bianca. Surely Rob could see how exhausted she looked. The way she sagged sideways in her seat tugged at my conscience. I felt like I could have worked harder to take care of her during that band battle business over the summer. I was about to leave Rob holding the remains of the conversation and sail down to ask how she was doing until two of her solid friends sauntered into the lecture hall, waving. Lynn Frampton dropped a breakfast sandwich on the desk nearest Bianca, and Olivia Adler set a coffee beside it.

"It means it's a good thing your Miss Brighton's got visible friends." Rob glanced to either side, then leaned closer before speaking in a hushed voice. "I'm here to keep an eye on someone, I'll let you guess who."

Before I could ask him what that he meant again, he shot upward through the ceiling. The side of Rob's head, including an ear and one corner of his hat, protruded from one of the acoustic tiles. Wilfred and then Ignacius had just started trying to straighten the leaning tower of paper into something more upright. They froze as a voice shrill enough to have come from a banshee sounded front and center in the lecture hall.

"Oh. My. Gawd!"

I turned slowly, expecting exactly what I saw before I'd even come full circle. The woman at the podium had dark hair, nearly black, and parted down the center. It hung to just past her shoulders, complementing the olive tone complexion of her face, which was crisscrossed with crow's feet and other fine lines. The only thing missing from that vision of Italian-American maternity was the brandishing of a wooden spoon.

"Fewmets." Wilfred spoke, but it was Ignacius who looked nervous. "That's Delilah Redford. She must be picking up the slack with Watkins in that coma."

"Can it, Wilfred," she snapped. "I'm so happy to see that some disembodied hoodlums made a huge mess of my lecture hall."

The woman cleared her throat, pointing up at us as she spoke again. "You three wise guys get your willpower under control, or so help me, I'll get even wiser on your collective behinds."

I smiled. This tirade was classic Mrs. Redford. Students chuckled, one of them actually slapping his knee before I recognized him as Tony Gitano. Of course, he'd side with the woman who fed him over the Nocturnal Lounge's ghosts. Who also fed him. Possibly more frequently since the resident Redcap had gone and gotten himself stuck in the Seelie side of the Under. My smile faded. I tried to swallow the sourness of my irony down as I floated down to help Ignacius steady the photocopied sheets on the table beside Mrs. Redford.

Bianca caught my eye and gave me a thumbs-up. Lynn shrugged, and Olivia squinted. I headed for the door along with my medium. She had another class in the hall next door after all. Wilfred and Ignacius were right behind me, and I couldn't blame them for wanting to create space between themselves and an angry medium.

Mrs. Redford's eyes might as well have been laser beams with the way they got all piercing. She shooed us as we went, mumbling something else about ghosts keeping their emotionally fueled incorporeal hands to ourselves. The dragon dad duo wafted out the door, but I went through the nearest wall just because I could.

Halfway through the summer, Bianca Brighton and I had managed to piss off a frighteningly powerful Extramagus. I hadn't left her alone for more than a few minutes at a time since then. I couldn't bear the thought of letting her die again. After all, I'd promised to protect her the night she'd done it the first time and become a medium in the first place.

"I've got no idea." Lynn hoisted a backpack that had to weigh half of what she did over one shoulder, then opened the door to the vestibule on her way outside. "I just don't know Professor Redford well enough to decide whether I think she's acting weird."

"She's not a professor, technically," said Bianca. "No advanced degree. Anyway, that makes two of us." She glanced at Olivia, who shrugged. "Okay, that's three." She turned her head my way, raising an eyebrow. "Horace?"

"You mean he's here?" Lynn smiled, then waved in my general direction. "Hi! Nice to— ahem— see you again." I liked Lynn, despite the snarky sense of humor. That was a common opinion amongst the corporeally challenged at PPC. She was one of the few people who actually remembered to thank the helper ghosts even though she couldn't see us.

I winked and said, "Back at you, Frampton," even though she couldn't hear me.

"Hoo, boy." Olivia's shoulders shook. Bianca also giggled, then yawned. "Drink your coffee, Bianca." The owl shifter raised her own cup. "We all need to get adjusted to the late shift."

"It's broken." Bianca turned the cup upside-down with an exaggerated pout because she'd already drunk it. "Hole in the top, tragic loss of hot caffeinated goodness." She pressed the back of one hand to her forehead. "Whatever will I do?"

"Get more, of course." Lynn pushed through the exterior door. "Hey, by the way, when do you two start working on that case with Mr. Ichiro again?"

"Next week." Olivia held the door for Bianca. "That's when the hospital says people who aren't on the guestlist can see Professor Watkins."

"What's the holdup been on that, anyway?" Lynn shook her head, striding off toward the dining hall. "With Professor Brodsky's trial in October, you'd think all the real adults would want everything investigated yesterday. I mean, Doctor Klein seems reasonable enough to understand that." The genius had a point as usual.

"I dunno." Olivia shrugged. "But it has something to do with licensing and law enforcement. It's them trying to get Mrs. Redford to go and check him out first because she's got better credentials than Bianca. But she never made it in, according to Mr. Ichiro. Something always comes up, and she cancels or doesn't make it in time before visiting hours are over."

"She manages to find time to fill in here on campus, but can't be bothered to go and actually see if he's brain dead for real or just out of his body." Bianca set her jaw. I knew she'd gotten her teeth into a loose thread. She wouldn't be letting it go any time soon, either. "Four months is way too long to avoid something like that."

"That seems odd for sure." Lynn scratched her head. "We're all going to have to put overtime hours on our thinking caps this semester, too, I guess. Just like the last one."

"Tell them I'm always wearing mine." I caught Bianca's eye and tipped the bowler hat I always kept materialized on my head. She relayed my message, and I smiled.

"Maybe you can get in to talk to Ed, then, Horace." Lynn reached for the dining hall door. "It's not like any of the rest of us are allowed to see him. It's like he's reverse grounded or something."

Only Bianca knew I'd already tried that. Every time I'd gone by, the house had been warded, and Mrs. Redford always said her son was either asleep or busy. We didn't bother mentioning it because there wasn't much we could do about it. Maybe we should have.

"It must suck for the poor kid. It's bad enough he can't see his brother until his mom okays it." Bobby Tremain pulled the door open, holding it for all three ladies. I got a little jealous. Doors were beyond the scope of my ability to move. I'd never been able to hold a door for Bianca, no matter how much I might like to.

"Well, you can't blame Mrs. Redford for being overprotective after Ed got spirited away to the Seelie court." Olivia ducked under Bobby's arm.

"This goes way beyond overprotective." Bianca sighed. "Irina says she pulled him from school, won't even let him come over for violin lessons. And Delilah's been friends with the Kazinskys for decades, too. You'd think she'd trust Irina and her Grandpa."

I sailed through the door Bobby had kept open, wondering exactly how bad Mrs. Redford's paranoia might be. I hung around with Bianca even though she wasn't keeping ghost-friendly company. My own irrational fears were a known quantity, after all.

But as it turned out, Delilah Redford's odd behavior wasn't paranoia at all. And my own fears were absolutely on point.

CHAPTER TWO

Bianca

I sat in the ICU waiting room at Rhode Island Hospital, trying not to look at the incorporeal people scattered around the hall. Two seats over from me, an elderly ghost woman knitted, her wooden needles making sounds only I could hear. No one else in the waiting area saw her. Well, that wasn't true.

I tried tuning her out so I could listen to Yoshi Ichiro negotiate with the Charge Nurse. Even though I'd wanted to come here the day after the Newport Battle of the Bands, legal technicalities had slowed my momentum. It had taken the rest of the summer for Mr. Ichiro to get my name on the court order with Mrs. Redford's, which would allow the lawyer to use any information I might gather from our visit in the case going to trial this October. I didn't catch everything he said, just the fact that we'd be allowed to visit the comatose Professor. Finally.

"The laws may stay the same, but everything changes this year." Mr. Ichiro turned his weary gaze toward the other solid student and me. He sat down, right in the knitting ghost. Ichiro-san's skills in the courtroom rocked, but he had no Psychic awareness at all. "Your schedule is one of those changes, Miss Adler. How is the nocturnal life going for you so far?"

"It's okay, I guess. But I still don't really understand the reason for it, sir." Olivia twirled a lock of her hair between two of her fingers, staring at the floor despite the respectful address. While Mr. Ichiro wasn't a full-time Professor with tenure, internships at his law firm were highly sought-after by Extrahuman Law students like Olivia Adler, the formerly diurnal owl shifter.

"Your internship requires that you complete the next two semesters of study as a nocturnal student, like Miss Brighton." Yoshi Ichiro glanced at me, his eyebrow raised before turning his gaze back to Olivia. "The judge presiding over Professor Brodsky's case works strictly in the night court, and I already have enough interns in the daytime for the rest of the year."

"I think this is a good thing." Horace leaned forward, putting his grinning face, monocle and all, between my classmate and me. "Poor Miss Adler's much less addled without all the medication changing her sleep schedule, don't you think?" My ghostly medium friend elbowed me. Well, not really. His elbow went straight through my shoulder. He rolled his eyes. "Sorry."

"After all the years you've been a ghost, you should know better, dude." I chuckled because Horace always pulled stunts like that just when I needed a laugh.

"Don't call me 'dude.'" Horace shook his head. I could just make out the sign that said "Nurse's Station" through his bowler hat. I thought he must be saving his energy for the encounter with Professor Watkins.

"Sorry, man." I winked, touching my fingers to my lips as I stared through my ghost buddy's chest at the platinum-haired woman in the seat beside mine. "And sorry, Olivia."

"No need to apologize for talking to your less-visible friends, Bianca." The owl shifter grinned. I wasn't sure why she leaned forward in her seat to peer at me. It wasn't like Horace could obstruct her view. Owl shifters could sometimes see ghosts but only while in their feathered forms. "I'd better get used to having ghosts around if I'm going nocturnal. The skeleton crew runs the campus after dark."

"If these legal eagles really want to get used to us, you had better tell them to get their own seats," said the knitting lady neither Olivia nor Mr. Ichiro could see. "I'm sick of being sat on, especially at this hour of the night."

"Um, Mr. Ichiro?" I glanced at the clock, the cup of pens on the Nursing Station's counter, the linen cart, everywhere but at the attorney I spoke to.

"I've done it again, haven't I, Miss Brighton?" He sighed and gripped the chair's armrests.

"Yeah, you have, sir." I gazed at my shoes until he chuckled softly.

I looked up to see Mr. Yoshi Ichiro, Attorney at Law, standing up and turning to face the seat he'd just vacated. He bowed his head and apologized to the ghostly knitter he'd been sitting on as the nurse arrived.

"I'll take you to see Professor Watkins now." The nurse spun on one clogged heel before I could get a good look at his name badge. The four of us followed even though the nurse thought he only escorted three visitors. Horace and I were the only ones dodging and turning to avoid walking through the hall's incorporeal denizens. I knew it made me look like an oddball, but I didn't care. The ghosts appreciated it, at any rate.

At first, it had been the weirdest thing ever, seeing all those people no one else can, even more anxiety-inducing than the pimples and hand-wringing of everyone else's puberty problems. But after ten years, I'd grown out of pimples and into being a medium. I hadn't done it alone. Since the minute I'd woken up in this very hospital, Horace had been with me, helping me make sense of all the extra, slightly transparent people I could see. If Horace hadn't gone to Delilah Redford, told her there was a brand new medium in town, I might have ended up at Butler Mental Hospital instead of Providence Paranormal College.

"You sure you're ready for what you might see in there?" Horace hovered close beside me. The other ghosts dodged him, making it easier for me to avoid them on my left.

"No, but the poor Professor's been stuck in here all summer," I mumbled. Only the nurse looked at me funny. Olivia and Mr. Ichiro expected me to have seemingly one-sided conversations. "This is the least I can do."

"But are you sure you're the medium who has to do it?" Horace peered at me from under the brim of his bowler hat.

"Yeah." I nodded. "I still don't know if Delilah's been in to see him. And if so, nothing he's said to her will help at this trial, anyway." Even though I'd taken pains to be quiet, I didn't dare mention Richard Hopewell, the Extramagus who'd been attacking my college and its students for over six months. According to the crew who hung out in the Nocturnal Lounge, the big bad Extramagus liked using magical surveillance gadgets. Lynn Frampton, the smartest girl at school, had a theory that he either couldn't or wouldn't spy with mundane devices. I took out my phone.

"Good idea." Olivia snapped her fingers to get Mr. Ichiro's attention once we'd all filed into the room. I waited until the nurse left before looking around to confirm my suspicions on the professor's condition. I typed everything I saw on Evernote, so I didn't have to risk anything I said getting picked up by a bug, magical or otherwise.

Professor Nathaniel Watkins looked like a waxwork in the bed. His pale, still hands and arms bristled with tubes embedded in his papery skin. Wires hung from electrodes clinging like morbid versions of stickers to his legs and neck. The hospital gown draped over his artificially rising and falling chest was a washed-out blue. I'd known he'd been in a coma and thought I was prepared to see him like this, but I still gasped and swallowed and blinked back tears. Psychics tended toward empathy, but my reaction was more extreme than usual. I took a deep breath and counted to four before looking around the room.

No flowers stood in vases. No balloons floated over the night-stand. No knick-knack or religious item or family photo sat propped on any of the stark, sterile surfaces. Only one faded, folded piece of cardboard lay flat on the windowsill on the other side of the bed. Olivia went and stood it up. I recognized it as the card Lynn Frampton and Bobby Tremain had insisted their entire pack sign and send back in June. But it was September now. It looked like no one besides the hospital staff had bothered with Professor Watkins since then.

I felt my hands tighten around the phone I still clutched and took three deep, cleansing, meditative breaths. I wasn't here to see the professor in the flesh, I'd come to see him in spirit. So I closed my eyes, and when I opened them again, narrowed my focus to concentrate on how he'd look to someone like me—a medium.

He wasn't dead. I'm not talking about the scientific sense, where the doctors look at an EKG's peaks and valleys or psychedelic blots of color on a brain scan. All those would look like Vacancy signs on the professor's body to almost anyone else. But the silver thread stretching between his midsection and a nearby wall told me he was just out to lunch, in a manner of speaking. Psychically projected. And that's what I tapped into Evernote, what Mr. Ichiro and Olivia read over my shoulder.

I caught Horace's eye, and he nodded. My partner plunged one arm through the wall behind the respirator up to his elbow. He smirked, moving his shoulder up and down, then locking his elbow before pulling his arm back through. A translucent and much healthier looking version of Nathaniel Watkins emerged, the silver thread at his middle shrinking as he got closer to the sickly form in the bed. I tapped away, describing and transcribing everything for the other solid people in the room.

"Don't even try to put me back in my body, Casper." The out-of-body professor gave my friend his best "you're failing this exam" stare. I knew it well. "Won't work. And I don't want visitors."

"The name's Horace." The ghost tipped his hat.

"I know who you are. Let go of my tether." Professor Watkins crossed his arms over his chest. Unlike ghosts, his limbs didn't pass through each other. That was promising. It meant his spirit form still remembered being in his body even though he could pass through inert barriers. "I won't go back inside the wall."

"You're an Astral Psychic so you know how this works, Professor." Horace shook his head. "You have to make an actual promise."

"Fine." Professor Watkins folded his arms over his chest, hovering in the air with his feet flexed. "I swear on my silver cord I'll stick around for this pointless chat."

"Good." Horace smiled and adjusted the goggles perched around the brim of his hat. Most of the other ghosts thought Horace was from the Victorian era, which sometimes gave him more authority over them. But he came clean with me about his love of Steampunk. "But you know, this chat is hardly pointless for poor Professor Brodsky. His trial's in October. We're told you have information that might exonerate him."

"Boo fricking hoo." Professor Watkins rolled his eyes. I noticed a slight movement under his body's eyelids to match. "I wish that old thing would work." He jerked his chin at his comatose form. "If it did, I'd finally get all the funding back for my department that he convinced Thurston to allocate to his."

"Oops." I shut my mouth around the end of the word I'd let slip. I typed out the rest of the thought so it couldn't get overheard. *I'd forgotten those two were academic rivals, worse than Lynn versus Blaine.* Ichiro-san and Olivia nodded.

"Listen, I know you don't care about Pavlo Brodsky personally." Horace tilted his head at me. "But I care about her. And you care about the College."

"What's that got to do with an old bigot finally going so completely nuts that he started exterminating vampires?" Watkins put his hands on his hips and leaned forward until he was right in Horace's face.

"Plenty." My friend kept his cool. "But the old bigot's not the real threat because his mind was compromised. Someone whammied him. You know that, don't you?"

"Yeah, I recommended a Psychic sleep-aid for him." The professor leaned back and looked sideways at each of us in turn. "I knew all about his insomnia." Nate's eyes glittered with something brittle, angry. "It's no excuse for crimes against extrahumanity. No excuse for trying to frame Thurston for them, either."

"But the Counselor here thinks it wasn't actually him." Horace nodded, reaching one hand out to indicate Mr. Ichiro. "You could help put the right person away, the one who's still messing with the school and everyone in it."

"I'm no fool, kid." He rolled his eyes. "There hasn't been anyone capable of Mind magic in Rhode Island since Ignacius Harcourt died taking down that Extramagus back before the Reveal. I'm giving you homework before I dismiss you. Check the Registry."

"Been there, done that, Bianca bought the T-shirt because I don't wear them." Horace's eyes jittered to the left, telling me he was about to take a leap of faith. "And by the way, that was not the last Extramagus, you know."

"I know. There was that one Henry and Dahlia fought against back in '89." Watkins waved one hand dismissively. "He didn't have Mind magic, by the way. But that was definitely the last one around these parts."

"You're wrong." Horace narrowed his eyes.

"What?" Nate Watkins blinked, his hand reaching absently for the silver thread at his midsection, a sign that Horace had caught him flat-footed.

"Guess you haven't heard since you've been hiding away in here." Horace's face went blank, grave. "Richard Hopewell's an Extramagus. Untithed changeling, too. Been posing as a garden-variety Fire Magus all this time, and he's getting himself involved in Faerie business. Courting the queen."

"Now, that's the biggest crock of bull I've heard this century." Watkins snorted. "Last century, too."

"Newport PD has proof Hopewell's attacked vampires with his registered Fire magic. We have four witnesses to him using Spectral magic in the Under, right in the queen's castle." Horace's lip curled in a sneer. "All we need to help with Brodsky's trial is reasonable doubt. If there's any hint, the tiniest clue that Richard's skill-set includes Mind magic and Brodsky was under his spell, you could help save an innocent man from a death sentence."

"Pavlo Brodsky's no innocent." Nate Watkins shook his head. "You should look into what he got up to back in Russia sometime. But still, it's true that he didn't torture and kill those poor vampires. I saw something that'll cast enough reasonable doubt to clear him, but nothing to incriminate Hopewell. I'm willing to help, I just don't know how. Even if I give you what information I have, there's no way my testimony will be valid in court."

"Why?" I typed the question, and Horace asked it.

"Because I can't get back in my body. I should be able to, but something's blocking me. And you know the courts only allow corporeal witnesses. Ghosts and other disembodied people can only help by pointing the authorities at hard evidence."

I peered at the professor's silver thread, unsure of what he meant by not being able to get back in. I couldn't see anything else occupying his corporeal form, but there was a faint bluish light around his incorporeal form that typically didn't surround the out-of-body set. I tapped all of this out on my phone, understanding that I'd have to do some research into it later.

"That must be awful." Horace shook his head. "So, there's no chance your information will lead to evidence?"

"No." Nate sighed, staring down at his body. "All I've got is my own eyewitness testimony about Hopewell giving Brodsky a magical device to help with his insomnia. My brother's another story. He has information on all of Rhode Island's Extramagi, family trees and the like, stored in a memory charm somewhere. That'd be some nuclear corroboration for a case against Hopewell."

"You didn't say 'had,' Nathaniel." Horace held up one finger, shaking it from side to side like a parent scolding a child.

"No, I didn't." Nate Watkins tilted his chin, his face a portrait of defiance. "Edgar's not dead."

"I tend to agree." Horace winked. "We spent the better part of the last month searching Rhode Island for his ghost. Yours, too. But if he isn't dead, where is he?"

"No idea." The corners of Nate's mouth turned down. "He should have shown up by now, with me in a coma all this time." He waved one hand at his body. "Then again, if there's a Hopewell Extramagus lighting the town up, I can hardly blame him for sticking with hiding. We've got something anyone involved in a power grab is going to want. The item's been hidden, but won't be for much longer."

The sound of the respirator filled the room as Olivia and Mr. Ichiro read along. I wished I could say something to Professor Watkins. He was a hard but effective teacher, one of the best at Providence Paranormal. I glanced around again at the bare room, hoping the reason he couldn't get back into his body wasn't that, deep down, he didn't want to. We certainly hadn't given him much encouragement to recover, psychically or otherwise.

Mr. Ichiro cleared his throat. "Perhaps the professor could tell us how to help him with this item."

"Even with your little electronic note-passing trick, I shouldn't." Professor Watkins grinned at me. "Nice job, by the way, Brighton. Way better than your Freshman coursework. Maybe I'm paranoid, but just in case I'm not—" He pointed his finger at numbers and letters on the phone, guided me to enter the address without speaking.

"We'll find your item there?" Horace peered at the street name right along with me. I wrinkled my nose as I realized it was in Olneyville. I hate Olneyville. It's where I had the near-death experience that made me a medium.

"Yes, Casper, if you do things the smart way." Professor Watkins snorted, his sarcasm approaching his legendary lecture hall levels. "There's a trunk in the attic at that address. You can't miss it. You'll need help, so bring the Umbral girl and that Gitano kid with you. If you only go with Brighton, you'll have big trouble."

"What about the police?" Horace translated my question.

"No cops or the people who own that building will torch the place, probably with you in it." He shook his head. "You'll need to go in hidden. That house is crawling with creatures you don't want your solid friends tangling with."

"Lion shifters?" Horace shuddered. I wondered whether they had anything to do with his own demise.

"Yeah. And maybe a few other things." Nathaniel Watkins smirked as he drifted back toward the wall he'd been hiding in. "Let Gitano take the lead, and don't let him make himself scarce until the other cats are in the bag. And find out how to get me back in my body. You're welcome." The last thing that vanished was that smirky half-smile. After that, the nurse cleared his throat from the doorway.

Mr. Ichiro gave Olivia and me a pointed look. It was about time we made ourselves scarce.

CHAPTER THREE

Horace

"But Tony. We really need your help." Bianca stood wringing her hands by the coffee station with Maddie May, the Umbral Magus.

"Yeah, and I distinctly remember you saying you were sick of sitting around waiting back in July." Maddie locked gazes with Tony Gitano. She put her hands on her hips so hard, the amulet that helped people like Bianca and ghosts like me remember her bounced against the front of her frilly black dress.

He turned his gaze away first. "Look, I said that about having a tango with the Extramagus, okay? This thing you want me to do is completely different. It's messing with Dad's business."

"Tell him you don't get how he can tell someone that powerful to just bring it and then chicken out over some of his own dad's goons." I exerted some of my energy to cool off the scalding coffee in the cup Bianca held. She took my advice, paraphrasing my idea.

"Do you have any idea how much worse my dad is than Richard Hopewell?"

"Last time I checked, the Gatto Gang hadn't committed any

crimes against extrahumanity." Maddie crossed her arms, her eyes narrowing as shadows gathered around her. I didn't blame her for being angry since said crimes had been targeting her fiancé.

"That you know of." Tony sighed, looking like a sail with the wind gone out of it. "Look, part of the reason Dad's so scary is that he's slipperier than an eel. Nothing sticks, he's made of Teflon, his Patronus is a stick of butter. I'm not going."

"I will hide us with Umbral magic, though." Maddie shook her head so hard, her curls bounced. "What could possibly go wrong?"

"You did not seriously just say those words? No, wait. You did." Tony wrinkled his nose, then stretched his mouth into a manic grin. "You're Maddie May, the girl who took a vampire on the lam from a Grim at dawn with nothing but an umbrella and a solar-powered calculator for a sun shield. Everyone knows you're dare-ier than the Daredevil." Tony stared into his coffee. "Look, Dad keeps all his operations warded ten ways from Sunday. He's got Magi and Faeries on his payroll. You won't get through."

"They will." Olivia Adler came down the stairs, her pace measured and mannish, almost like marching. "I'm going with them." She pulled a pair of wire-rimmed spectacles from her pocket and brandished them like a dagger. They looked magipsychically enhanced. "I'll check for wards with these. Then, I get them to open the door. A piece of paper with Mr. Ichiro's letterhead on it should do the trick better than Doctor Who's psychic paper."

"No. Don't even show your faces over there. Those guys eat lawyers for breakfast." Tony crossed his arms over his chest, nostrils flaring as he tilted his head and leveled his gaze at the owl shifter. "There's no point in even checking for wards. I can already tell you if my dad owns it, he wards it. Unless it's a trap."

"But wards that extensive take time. How can your dad ward properties he just closed on yesterday?" Bianca had beaten me to the punch on that one. She was way sharper than the other solids gave her credit for. They didn't understand that she wasn't staring off into space half the time, just looking at all of us incorporeals. "Even for the most powerful Magi, wards take time and concerted effort. The same goes for Faeries, even the Pure kind."

"Wait." Tony tapped one finger against his temple. "I can't believe I'm actually asking this question. What's the address of this house?"

Bianca rattled it off and waited. Tony's face paled except for two feverish looking spots high on his cheekbones. Maddie rolled her eyes and mouthed the words "fraidy cat" behind her hand at Bianca. Olivia clenched one fist at her side, glaring at Maddie. I knew the Umbral Magus was the fearless type, but she probably shouldn't piss Olivia off. I'd seen that girl go off on Lane Meyer over the summer. Owls aren't just cute fluffy birdies like everyone wants to think. They're predatory, territorial, and protective.

"Well, I know where it is now, so like it or not—" Olivia stepped closer to Tony, a vindictive little smirk on her lips as she approached him. He locked gazes with her as though the other two women in the Lounge were as invisible to him as I was.

"Yeah, okay." Tony looked like he was about to either kiss her or spit hairballs. "We can get in there. But we have to do it tonight."

"So you'll help us?" Bianca smiled.

"Yeah, sure, fine, whatever." Tony stepped away from the owl shifter. "Bianca, Maddie, and me. And whatever ghost the whisperer wants to bring. No owls allowed." Tony ran one hand over his head, ruffling his hair. "But all I can do is get them to open the door and stop paying attention to you guys for about an hour. You're on your own for the rest."

And that's how we all ended up back in Olneyville.

"Funny story." Tony sauntered down the street, a Bluetooth earphone clipped over his left ear. Brilliant. Also sneaky. I couldn't blame people like Blaine Harcourt for not trusting the cat shifter. "A medium, a Magus, and a cat shifter walk into a Gatto Gang safehouse. They do it without bringing any food."

"So, what's the punch line?" Bianca asked, whispering into her phone so Tony could hear without them breaking Maddie's Umbral cover.

"Them. Their tickets, actually. That's what gets punched." Tony turned a corner, his face glowing red in the neon light of a garish sign above a battered chrome storefront. It bore the words New York System. "That's the only punch line you get unless you send something more appealing to a goombah's senses than a Trojan Cat to the door. I'll be back."

Bianca, Maddie, and I watched him enter the store, approach the counter, and shout what I assumed was a food order at the chef. Well, maybe "chef" was too fancy a term. The guy in the stained apron at the griddle was massive, his arms so long and broad that thirty of the hot dog rolls fit all down his left one. I squinted at him, wishing I could see auras or magic to confirm my guess about him.

"Bear shifter?" Bianca glanced at Maddie.

"No. Bigger and not nearly so hairy." The Umbral magus gestured at the griller. "Rhino, maybe or elephant. His magic's got no hint of water, or I'd say hippo."

"You've really come a long way with your studies, Maddie." Bianca grinned at her friend.

"I owe it all to Lynn." Maddie shrugged. "She's the one who started the summer online course trend, and she knows all the best study habits. The only Tinfoil Hatters who didn't take any were Lane and the other guys in Night Creatures. But can you blame them?"

"Of course not." Bianca chewed her bottom lip. "And Fred Redford."

"Well, you can't get on the Internet from the Under." Maddie shook her head, then pointed at Tony, who'd made a second order. "Wow. How many goons do you think are in that house, Bianca?"

"No idea. But Tony must know what he's doing, right?" Bianca looked at me, and I winked. Any reassurance I could give her would help. She tended to overthink things when she believed she was in over her head.

"He's one crafty cat, I'll give him that." Maddie sighed. "But if the place is too packed, we might have trouble. My magic doesn't do a thing to cover us if we bump into anyone or anything."

"Yeah, I remember." Bianca clasped her hands together. "Interacting with nouns breaks the shadows. I promise to be careful."

"So does too much bright light." Maddie glanced at Bianca. "You sure you can handle this? I'd never have thought you were the sneaky type."

"I'm not." Bianca sighed. "But Professor Watkins said I had to go with you to get this thing, whatever it is. Horace, too. So there must be some Psychic or ghostly element to what we're after that a Magus like you won't be able to handle."

I wished I knew what Bianca really thought and felt about taking this risk and whether she shared my suspicion about the professor's request. He'd hinted that there might be more than Gattos guarding the place. The situation looked much worse than we'd originally thought, and if things went too far south, we might not be able to handle them.

We hadn't crossed the line from partnership to Possession, which was supposed to be more like sharing a body than one of us taking it over from the other. Possession was a two-way street unless one of the partners was stronger than the other. We were about evenly matched. Only a ghostly medium and a living Psychic medium could do it, too. But I'd never worked up the courage to ask about trying it, even though it felt like Bianca and I had known each other forever.

If we bonded that way, I'd know all of her thoughts and feelings, and she'd get the same from me. On top of that, our partnership would become permanent, and at exactly the same time she would discover my secret. If she didn't have the same one, she might not want to be partners or even friends anymore, and after Possession, she wouldn't have any way out besides death.

Before I could start dwelling on all that potential drama, Tony sauntered out of the New York System joint. I glided along in the invisible wake behind the hidden girls, glad I couldn't smell the oniony, beefy, and spicy wieners from inside Tony's brown paper bag. Remembering was bad enough. The one time I'd gotten drunk, I binged on New York System. Worst night of my physical life.

I stopped reminiscing to stare at the house Tony stopped in front of. The siding's blue paint peeled like my skin used to three days after a blistering sunburn. The front door bore pockmark scars and squares where No Trespassing signs used to be. If I squinted, I could see their vestiges. Sometimes, signs had a way of clinging to the solid world like ghosts themselves.

Tony Gitano set his lips in a casual smirk that avoided his eyes like the plague. Those were flat and severe. When he knocked, he blinked, and a feverish glint replaced the flatness in his eyes. His classmates liked joking about him being a coward, but once he found himself in danger, Tony had a gutter punk variety of bravery. Anyone who mistook it for false bravado might get a nasty surprise. The door opened scant seconds later.

"Yeah, kid. Whaddaya want?" A Gatto goon I recognized from over the summer as Paul "the Maul" stood in the doorway. He occupied way too much space for Maddie and Bianca to get through.

"Made a wiener run," said Tony. "Thought I'd drop some here while I was in the neighborhood."

"Huh." Paul put his hands on his hips and looked down his nose. "And what else? It's never just one thing with you."

"Wanted to check out these new digs." Tony pretended to stifle a yawn. "Turns out, they're not worth all the time and effort Pops went to to get them."

"You can't be serious." Paul grabbed Tony by the lapels and shook him, rattling the bag of wieners.

"Composolutely and absotively serious." Tony's smile reminded me of a dagger.

"Get your Hello Kitty tail in here, and I'll show you something serious." Paul dragged his boss's unfavorite son through the door, turning to drop him on a foyer bench before heading back to close the door. That gave the girls the time and space they needed to hightail it inside.

I floated through the wooden panel after it closed, intending to stay near Maddie and Bianca as they headed up the stairs. I spared Tony a backward glance. His pupils went vertical as his gaze locked on mine. His smile was wide and genuine this time, even though Paul berated him about disrespecting the other Mr. Gitano.

Before I could investigate my suspicion that a cat shifter who shouldn't be able to see me actually did, a muffled creak at the top of the stairs reminded me of why I was really here. I followed my partner and left Tony's catty hinkiness for another time.

CHAPTER FOUR

Bianca

We made it through the door just in time, but getting to the top of the stairs was another story. Maddie and I had to dodge out of the way when one of the Gattos left the second-floor bathroom and almost stepped on my toe. To make matters worse, Horace was still heading up the stairs, one ghostly finger tracing the ornately carved antique banister. The goon stopped as my ghost friend traipsed right through him, shivering. It'd figure that the shifter who happened to be Psychically sensitive was the one in the restroom.

I shook a finger at Horace, rolling my eyes and feeling for all the world like he should have known better. But then again, maybe the old-timey decor had distracted him. He loved anything Victorian, which was why he always had the bowler hat and goofy goggles. I couldn't stay annoyed at him for that.

Luckily for us, the goon just went along on his way downstairs, making a beeline for one of the paper bags of wieners Tony had dropped on the bench in the hall. Apparently, the gut-busting food was more likely to kill a member of the big-cat Mafia than curiosity. Good for us, and hopefully Tony, too.

We tip-toed all the way to the end of the hall because that's where we expected to find the stairs to the third floor in a house like this. We went up, turning the corner after the first half-flight. The ceilings up here were all slanted, with cracked horsehair plaster and round windows. And finally, we saw the way to the attic Professor Watkins had mentioned. Behind a door, of course.

"Well, at least it's not one of those noisy drop-ladders." Maddie punctuated her whisper with a shrug. She peered at a spot near my left shoulder, then caught my eye and raised an eyebrow.

"Yeah, he's here." I looked past Maddie. "Do you have enough energy for turning a doorknob, Horace?"

"Give me half a moment." Horace straightened the brown jacket he always wore, tilted his hat, then adjusted his waistcoat and tie. After that, he cracked his knuckles before producing a pair of white gloves from up his sleeves.

I watched, completely aware that all of his preparations had nothing to do with his clothes. Ghosts appeared how they imagined they should. Their appearance was an expression of their identity and skill, and all of their accessories had something to do with their strengths and talents. Without the ability to breathe or count heartbeats, ghosts needed other ways to concentrate and gather energy. Horace was focusing his will, just like I did with meditation, counting, and calming breaths.

All ghosts need some kind of emotional force to affect the solid world. Only experienced or exceptionally strong-willed spirits could focus enough to do something as specific as turning a doorknob. All of Horace's tools, personal items, and clothing were symbols and functioned as a way to channel his energy. As a ghostly medium, Horace had more of those than most other spirits. I knew it'd be the same for me after I died someday.

Maddie elbowed me in the ribs. I rolled my eyes and tapped my wrist. Even though no one else was on the third floor with us, I didn't want to make any more noise than we had to. The Umbral Magus's impatience could get dangerous if we didn't get a move on soon.

Horace pointed one finger at the cut-glass doorknob, and I watched as his entire hand went nearly opaque. Maddie clutched her arms, shivering a little as our breath came out all misty even though it had been warm when we got up there. Ghosts exerting their will always dropped the ambient temperature. But this time, it got colder than the Nocturnal Lounge during cleaning night, when fifteen of my incorporeal helpers lifted the furniture so I could vacuum.

My eyes stung when I blinked, and the inside of my nose prickled when I inhaled. I couldn't feel my fingertips or the end of my nose. Looking at Maddie, I knew she experienced similar effects. Instead of shivering, she practically quaked. And she was from Vermont. Horace turned the knob, long-stilled hinges finally moving as the door unlatched and swung outward. I grabbed Maddie by the elbow because she seemed too distracted to come along on her own. I moved her just in time, too.

Another spirit floated through the ceiling, this one in raggedy remnants of clothing like a tatterdemalion. Deformity defined its body, giving it the appearance of being threadbare in places and nearly solid in others. I'd never seen one before, but I knew this particular ghost had lost too much of themself and gone wraith.

Maddie and I took the stairs behind the door two at a time on our toes, a real feat for the Magus since she was five foot nothing and wearing stompy Goth boots. At least I had long legs, soft shoes, and had taken ballet class all the way up until I became a medium.

Once we'd reached the attic, I whipped out my key-fob. At one end was a little LED flashlight, which I switched on and swung around the room. The chest we were after squatted in the far corner, its hump-backed shape unmistakable though a drop-cloth shrouded it.

"We've got to get out of here." Horace's voice sounded almost whiny, tired and strained. He looked a little faded, too. Drained energy problems were the price for a ghost of interacting with anything solid. I knew he'd get better once we got back to campus, where his contract was. But I didn't have the strength myself to prop him up much with my own Psychic energy while in this kind of danger.

"I know." I reached for the drop-cloth, pulled it off to reveal metal handles on either end of the box. After that, I felt colder, and the room seemed a bit brighter. I'd broken Maddie's Umbral cloaking spell.

"No time to open it, just grab and go!" Maddie barreled past me, making a fist around one handle. I took up the other, and we lifted. She paused, and I felt a faint warm tingle. She nodded, and I knew she'd pulled her Umbral shadows back around us.

The trunk didn't weigh much, it was just cumbersome. I wondered how we'd get it down all those stairs without bumping anything. We didn't manage that. The old chest clunked against one wall halfway down from the attic. Maddie redid her magic, and I held my breath the rest of the way, waiting for the sound of Gatto goons coming up here to investigate the noise.

I expected to see the wraith back on the third floor, but it was gone. They could be unpredictable, but once a wraith decided to chase something, that's what they did until whatever anchor kept them from moving on limited their range. Ghosts had to stay within a certain radius of anchors unless they had contracts listing either a set of locations or duties. But just before we got to the stairs heading down to the second floor, the wraith burst through from the ceiling. It had been following us from inside the attic.

Maddie wanted to keep on going, but I stopped her without explanation. She knew I could see things she couldn't. After all,

Umbral Magi were no strangers to the idea of the selectively seen. Running through a wraith was bad news for a Magus. Whatever spells they had going would stop, and we couldn't afford to lose her shadows. We were literally stuck between a wraith and the Gattos.

"Hey, shady shade!" Horace waved his hands over his head, nearly knocking his bowler hat askew. "Why don't you pick on someone of your own incorporeality?"

I blinked, mouth dropping open as Horace's hands erected a pair of birdies I never imagined him using. I swallowed the laugh that tried to tumble out. The wraith understood the gesture's intent even if it didn't get the context. It headed right for Horace, leaving Maddie and me free to navigate the stairs.

We trundled down, going as fast as we dared with the trunk. We made it down the flight and the second-floor hall, stopping at the head of the last set of stairs. And then, both of us nearly doubled over with laughter, not even caring that the magic cloaking spell dropped away. We didn't need it.

Tony Gitano sat on the hall bench, grinning up at us like the cat that had eaten an entire pet shop worth of canaries. He nudged an unconscious Paul next to him with one Converse-clad foot, prodding a long and droning snore from the goon's grease-smeared mouth. And then, Tony got up and opened the front door, presenting a safe passage to us with a one-handed flourish.

Maddie paused to redo her cloaking magic. It wouldn't do to be seen leaving a Gatto Gang safe house with something we'd more than technically stolen. After that, we headed down and out onto the porch, then the sidewalk. Tony shut the door as he followed, his gaze on something across the street. He looked away before I noticed Horace leaning against a lamppost over there. The wraith was nowhere in sight.

The group of us walked along in silence until I finally couldn't stand it anymore. I had to know, so I glanced up to where Horace floated ahead and slightly above us.

"What happened to that wraith back there?" I kept my voice quiet enough not to break Maddie's spell, but loud enough that she could hear me.

Maddie stifled a gasp as she finally understood why I stopped her upstairs. Horace continued on quietly for a few moments.

"I guess it's anchored to the building," he finally said. "I went outside, and it just beat at this weird, round window, unable to follow."

"Well, that's lucky," I explained Horace's taunt and his answer to Maddie, then turned back to my partner. "Don't do something that risky again, especially not after something strenuous like opening a door." Horace nodded. Maddie didn't.

"How can a ghost do something risky?" Her brow furrowed. "They're already dead, right?"

"Do you know where wraiths come from, Maddie?" I adjusted my grip on the trunk's handle.

"I bet it's not something that happens when a mommy wraith and a daddy wraith love each other very much, huh?" Maddie chewed on her bottom lip.

"No." I shook my head, then looked Horace right in the eyes. "It's when a ghost gets so drained, he forgets himself."

"Oh." Maddie narrowed her eyes, footsteps stamping more stompily than usual. "Don't you ever do that kind of thing again, Horace. Taunting a wraith is serious business," she said to thin air. I appreciated her sentiment and effort, even if her aim was off.

My phone beeped. I pulled it from my pocket one-handed to find a text from Tony. *Where are we bringing the unmatched luggage?*

Dennison place. Blaine, Al, and Ismail all have to check it out before opening.

"See you later, then." Tony tapped his Bluetooth earphone. He turned the corner into an alley. No matter how much I peered and squinted after him, there was no trace of the cat shifter. But cat shifters couldn't do magic. So how did he vanish?

"I really wish he and Blaine would just bite the bullet and get along already." Maddie sighed, yanking on a curl with her thumb and forefinger and letting it spring free. "It really makes everything we have to do ten times harder."

"I might have missed something, but why do the two of them refuse to occupy the same building?" Blaine had always mostly ignored Tony up until after Spring Break.

"I don't even know, really." Maddie shrugged. "I wish someone had the answer to that question besides Blaine himself."

"That's simple." I blinked as the ghost of Wilfred Harcourt began pacing me. "Blaine blames Tony for my death, of course." I translated for Maddie.

"Well, crap." Before we could discuss further, we reached the side street where the sedan our dragon shifter friend had provided, idled, waiting for us. "We'll have to talk about this later."

We never got the chance.

CHAPTER FIVE

Horace

"Insulin, kid." I pointed at Bianca's satchel.

"I know." She yawned.

"What did he say?" Maddie sat in the seat across from her, peering all around Bianca.

"He reminded me that I need to take my medicine." Bianca pulled the seatbelt across her body and fastened it with a click.

"Oh yeah. For your diabetes?" Maddie side-eyed the safety strap like it was an annoying little brother, then shrugged and put her seatbelt on, too.

"I've got type one." She rummaged in her bag, producing the small, zippered case she kept her medicine in.

Maddie smirked at the cover. Bianca had dropped some extra money to get one with a fancy art print on the outside.

"Hey, is that Son of Man by Magritte?" Maddie leaned forward to get a better look.

"No, Son of Man's the one with the apple under the hat." Bianca pulled an insulin syringe out of the case, then passed it to Maddie. "It's still Magritte, but this is Man in a Bowler Hat. You can tell because this one has a dove. He painted this twenty years after the other."

"You have a thing for bowler hats or just fine art?" Maddie smiled, handing back the case.

"Neither." Bianca chuckled. She set the case on the seat beside her, then reached under her shirt with the syringe. After making the little squeak she nearly always did when injecting, she pulled her hands out from under and tucked the now empty syringe away. "I got it because that painting always reminds me of Horace, who makes sure I take my insulin."

"Is it the hat or the dove?" Maddie leaned back, fiddling with her seatbelt.

"A little of both." Bianca's smile was wearier than I liked, even though her words made me remember what it was like to get butterflies in the stomach.

I stuck my head through the divider to check the digital clock in the middle of the dashboard up front. Eight-thirty. I went back again, but before I could do more than open my mouth, Bianca spoke.

"He's going to tell me I'm late for dinner." Bianca leaned back against the cushioned leather seat.

"I'll take care of that." Maddie pulled out her phone and started tapping.

I floated around and looked over the Magus' shoulder, then relaxed as I saw who and what she texted. I know it seems odd, the idea that a ghost could be tense or relaxed, but our bodies are subject to our will, which comes from what and who we care about most. For me, that was Bianca Brighton.

When the Psychics who kept us in contact with the living world didn't look after themselves properly, ghosts could make a serious ruckus. Unlike moving something on purpose, random acts of ghostly chaos come naturally. They're reflexive, like our incorporeal selves following the laws of physics while riding in a car or not falling through a chair while sitting on it. Those things were so ingrained in the human experience that they came as second nature.

The car slowed, turning as it headed up the Dennison driveway. I concentrated and unhinged myself from the car's momentum, rushing ahead and into the lower level of the rambling house. That renovated basement was where the Tinfoil Hatters met to discuss Extramagus concerns while off-campus. It made sense. Josh the werewolf was Alpha of that motley pack. It didn't hurt that his mother headed the Extrahuman Crime Unit for the Providence Police Department and his dad was head of PPC's Campus Security.

Like typical young adults, the pack didn't often ask for help from their parents and Professors. The older set knew about the situation. Maybe they already had some kind of plan to act out. If so, they hadn't found success so far. But, being a ghost, I had a different perspective. I'd come to suspect that the older generation had been the ones to mess things up in the first place. That'd explain their inaction.

There was a sort of karma to magic and the people who lived in and around it: coincidence. Extrahumans tended to fall into patterns of success or failure. They could only nudge the direction of the world in small ways. Once they drifted to one side, getting back across to the other approached impossibility. The pack's parents, aunts, and uncles were stuck on the sides they'd chosen decades ago. Some of those were obvious, like Josh's parents. Others, like Blaine's mother Hertha, not so much.

At any rate, the Dennison place was about as secure as it could get, even more so than the Harcourt mansion over in Newport. Neither were warded against ghosts, though. I glanced over my shoulder as I barreled through the wall. Blaine's two dads were in mostly invisible attendance right along with me.

"Um, Horace?" Wilfred's ghost reached out as he tried to stop me as I passed by. It didn't work. I may not have been dead as long as Rob was, but I had ten years of incorporeal experience on the ghost formerly known as a dragon.

"Not now." I waved my hand at Wilfred like he was a fly instead of an ex-dragon and watched the only garden-variety human in the place put away her phone.

Lynn stood up, cracking her knuckles. She headed to the door with her mate Bobby. I heard them murmuring about testing Bianca's blood sugar before she even walked through the door. Those Tinfoil Hatters took care of each other. It's one of the reasons I liked them all so much.

I headed back toward the Dragon Family. "Okay, Wil. What's up?"

"Stop calling me that." Wilfred rolled his eyes. I peered through him, trying not to smirk as I watched Blaine make almost the same face while talking to the Psychic vampire, Henry Baxter.

"Fine. Wilfred." I nodded, unable to ultimately chase the ghost of a grin from my not-all-there features. "What's up?"

"I want to know how long it might take me to move on."

Ignacius' peal of laughter had us both turning our heads.

"What's so funny?" Wilfred's fists went through his hips instead of on them as he'd clearly intended. He barely noticed.

"Dragon business has a way of sticking around." Ignacius jerked his chin at Blaine, who resembled his step-dad Wilfred in mannerism and his biological father in form and feature. The fire dragon's ghost met my gaze with a piercing glare. "You tell him how it is, Horace. You've avoided it for too long."

"Fine." I turned to Wilfred. "Some ghosts stick around for five minutes. Others, more like fifty years." I held up one finger. "That's because if you started something, you stick around to see the end of it." I held up another finger. "You might not go anywhere until your kid hatches, possibly longer." The door opening distracted me.

Maddie escorted a yawning Bianca over to one of the stools

by the bar. True to her word, Lynn brandished a glucometer with all the trimmings at Bianca, who held out her hand like a good sport. I watched my medium sit down before turning my attention back to Wilfred.

"But if that's the case, how come there are ghosts who never had kids when they were alive?" Wilfred tilted his head. "That little old lady ghost I met right after I died said she was a spinster. So, what kept her from moving on?"

"Two things might have a hold on someone like her. One of them is contracts. If we make them, we don't move on until we honor them." I glanced from Wilfred to Ignacius and back again, figuring number four had something to do with why at least two of us were still here. "And then there's the mushy stuff. True love, destiny, all that jazz. Sometimes, we stay put because coincidence makes us wait for who and what our hearts need. That goes quadruple for you dragons, who get hitched to make the strongest offspring and not like those two." I waved a hand at where Josh leaned against the wall, on one arm, nose to nose with Nox Phillips, his mate.

At the bar, Bianca sipped soda from a glass, then leaned one side of her face heavily on one of her hands. She didn't look as relaxed or alert as I would have liked, but some color had come back to her cheeks. Corners of stray papers stopped fluttering as her improving condition calmed me.

"So, I can't move on and get away from this dumpster fire until my egg hatches, or I find true love?" Wilfred didn't stare daggers at Ignacius, he glared claymores.

"You're stuck playing second fiddle here, too, airbag." Until Ignacius snorted, I hadn't thought it was possible for a fire dragon's ghost to make smoke rings. Something must have given his energy a boost, but I couldn't figure out what.

"Second fiddle?" Wilfred rolled his eyes again. "That's rich. How long did it take you to even consummate your marriage with Hertha?"

"My sex life is none of your business!" Ignacius exuded more ersatz smoke than I thought possible. Not Blaine, then. Something else that had to do with mating.

"More like boring. Ancient history." Wilfred snorted. "What did it take, a hundred years for you two to make Blaine's egg?"

"Can you two please settle down?" Bianca's face paled again as she poked it between the two arguing ghosts. "A little peace and quiet would rock right about now." Her eyelashes fluttered above the circles under her eyes, which were just a shade darker than her lavender hair.

"We need to have this out sooner or later, Miss Brighton." Wilfred put his hands on his hips again.

"The lady asked for a break." I got in his face, literally. "Go blow off steam somewhere else, Willie."

As I leaned back, I peered at Wilfred. He gaped and blinked more like a fish out of water than a guy who used to turn into a football-field-sized dragon.

"You heard the man." Ignacius' smug tone made my eyes go from wide to narrow in under sixty nanoseconds.

"Cool your jets, Iggy." I glared at each of them in turn. "I'm the ghost with the most here, and this isn't the time or place for your dramafest."

"Well, Wilfred's right. There should be one eventually." I sighed.

Bianca put one hand out, brushing lightly against the closest approximation to my forearm. It tingled. I expected that; we were both Mediums, after all. It didn't lessen the impact of the gesture or the exertion of her Psychic ability to interact with me by touch. Even exhausted, she cared enough to comfort me.

"Right." Bianca nodded. "So some other time, you two need to have a talk. I'll help if you want."

"Hoo, boy." Olivia peered over Bianca's shoulder, shaking her head. "Ghostly misbehavior again? Too distracting for what we've got to do." The owl shifter jerked her chin at Maddie, who stood next to the box we'd liberated from the Gatto safehouse like a dusky-skinned Goth Vanna White.

"Fine." Wilfred gave Bianca a nod. "I'll head out, do some work at the Nocturnal Lounge."

My respect for Wilfred grew even after the condescending little golf wave he flapped in Ignacius' general direction. Whatever beef the two dragon ghosts had with each other, Olivia was right. It was too distracting. My eyebrows scrunched together, and I opened my mouth, about to ask Bianca why an owl shifter in human form seemed to know what was going on with the nobody crew. But Lane Meyer and his literal band of vampires opened the door, bearing a big bag of takeout from the Moon Star Chinese restaurant. I let Bianca eat her lo mein in peace.

"So, can we open the box?" Kimiko Ichiro was probably the most curious member of Tinfoil Hat. Tanuki were like that.

"After I eat, silly." Bianca twirled noodles around her fork and ate them, chewing thoughtfully.

"And you really have no idea at all what's in it?" Blaine crossed his arms over his chest, raising an eyebrow.

"Nope." Maddie shrugged. "We'll find out soon enough."

"But can't one of the ghosts just stick his head in and check?" Lane pulled a bag of blood from the fridge behind the bar, popped the top, and poured it into a red plastic party cup.

"No." Bianca shook her head. "Well, technically, Horace can. But it's not a good idea." I watched her eyes move from one face to the next. The left corner of her mouth tilted, making the faint scar at the temple on that side come out of hiding. "The box might be booby-trapped against ghosts. The only one we saw in the Olneyville house was a wraith. I have no idea how the poor thing got that way. But a trap on this box could explain it."

"Yeah, now I remember." Olivia cradled a cup of tea between her hands. "Certain magic or Psychic energies can harm incorporeal people. Wraiths are damaged ghosts." Olivia shivered. "You really saw one in there?"

Bianca just nodded, shutting her eyes as she chewed another mouthful of thin, yellow noodles. I didn't blame her. That wraith had been a total wreck, pitiable.

Bianca set down her fork, wiped her hands, then knelt on the floor next to the box. She took five deep breaths, and I counted five seconds on each inhale and exhale. When she pressed her palms together, I watched, waiting for the flash that always came when she focused her Psychic energy on an item. A stream of lavender light flowed from her fingertips to the seam around the trunk's lid.

Blaine squinted, his pupils going vertical and reptilian. Henry nodded. Bobby stepped in front of Lynn while Nox did the same for Josh. Lane put one hand over his mouth while his bandmates looked on. Olivia blinked. And the box clicked, then rusty ingots creaked as the lid reared up on its hinges all by itself.

I rushed upward so I could peer down at the flat, beige rectangle at the bottom of the box. Bianca looked up, meeting my translucent gaze with her solid one. I nodded, and she reached out with both hands, scooping up the manila envelope between them. Turning it over, she unwrapped the red string from the two tan discs holding the whole thing closed. Once unfastened, she reached inside and pulled out an unfolded sheet of paper, eight by ten.

"Encoded." Bianca shook her head, then turned the paper around so everyone could see the characters in neat block lettering filling it from edge to edge. She handed the paper over to Kimiko, then shuffled back to her seat at the bar and the half-finished plate of lo mein.

"Is that Latin?" Lynn's eyebrows could have shaken hands. "It almost looks like Latin."

"Italian mixed with something else, actually." Kimiko shook her head. "Some other things, I should say. I'm not sure what, either."

"Let me see." Blaine peered over his mate's shoulder. "Hebrew, maybe? No. I'm stumped. And there are numerals." He sighed. "Do you guys want the good news or the bad news?"

"Hit us with the bad first, Trogdor." Josh had moved to the other side of the billiards table. Nox peered over his shoulder, staring at the paper. Her eyes crossed slightly, and she looked away.

"Well, it's definitely a doozie of an encryption. Probably made by more than one person, too, which fits with the theory that the Watkins brothers know something." Blaine cleared his throat. "I can't crack this at all. It's got magic and psychic on it, too, so I can't hack it with my energy alone."

"Okay." Josh gave Blaine one sharp nod. "Good news time."

"I think Kim can crack it. Translation-wise, I mean."

"Woah, dude." Kimiko shook her head. "Not alone, I can't. I don't know enough Italian. I'm going to have to work with Tony on this."

"Fewmets!" One of Blaine's fists crashed into the palm of his other hand. "No such thing as good news." Smoke drifted up from the dragon shifter's nose.

"We all know how you feel about the cat-man." Josh shook his head. "If our code guru says she needs his help, you'll have to deal with it. Maybe it's time for you two to bury the hatchet."

"Whatever." Blaine collected his jacket from the coat rack, then headed for the door.

"This could take weeks," Kimiko called after him. The door slammed. "Blaine's going to have to get along with Tony, eventually."

"You're not wrong." Lynn Frampton sighed and pulled out her phone, then patted Kimiko's shoulder.

"Tony knows now." Olivia tucked her own phone back in her pocket. "He's got class all night, though."

I would have waited to hear what else they talked about, but Bianca lied and said she had to work. I went with her, of course.

Back in her room, she fell into bed without even taking off her shoes.

I put that right for her, at least. It was still warm enough for her sandals, and nudging a couple of straps was nowhere near as taxing as turning a doorknob. Then, I tucked the sheet and the bedspread around her shoulders. She deserved so much more than anything I'd be able to do for her, or than the others could imagine she'd need. She was one of those people others feel they can say anything to. The kind who hide whatever burdens they have behind a compassionate facade like those brightly-beaded curtains people used to hang in doorways.

But Bianca Brighton was close to breaking, and if that night was any indication, the situation was about to get even worse.

CHAPTER SIX

Bianca

I stood at the back of the lecture hall, trying not to stare at the woman in front of the class. I'd never seen Delilah Redford actually do anything this academic, which made her seem almost like a different person. She used all those vocabulary words they put on college entrance exams. Even her nasal voice and flat-voweled Rhode Island accent had diminished to nearly nothing. She sounded like she was straight outta Hogwarts instead of straight outta Federal Hill.

It was more than a little unsettling to watch Mrs. Redford's teacherly persona. The creepiness factor rivaled Unseelie court history with Lady Amalthea, a Goblin Duchess whose voice sounded like a squeaky wheel. Even an elderly Goblin's voice wasn't as bad as the nails-on-chalkboard sound coming from above the ceiling. I averted my eyes and swallowed my curiosity, not wanting to let Mrs. Redford or my classmates down. I'd been called here to fix the ghostly prankster's wagon, after all.

Glaring up, I scanned the scalloped tin ceiling for the incorporeal culprit, Rob. He'd been even more of a problem on campus than usual since Mrs. Redford filled in for Professor Watkins. Or maybe it had more to do with Fred Redford, her elder son and the first Redcap knight in the Sidhe Queen's court in over a hundred years, being off doing his mandatory time in the Under. Rob was supposedly a Redford family ghost. Changes in the family dynamic had a history of affecting them.

I took a deep breath and focused, targeting my energy at the spot I'd last seen the pesky poltergeist. And I didn't want to point but had to. The question arose in my mind again. Why couldn't Mrs. Redford handle this problem herself? Maybe she thought it undermined her academic authority, doing stuff that fell under my job description. After all, this wasn't a course about ghosts or mediums. Ghost wrangling in front of an audience who couldn't see them wouldn't make for a good demonstration exercise. But Rob was easily the oldest and most powerful ghost I'd ever encountered. Without my little pal Ed Redford, who was the Colonial ghost's medium, I couldn't expect him to honor simple requests. Rob wouldn't come down from there unless I reeled him in like a sport fisherman catching a shark. So, that's exactly what I did.

Paper and fabric rustled as the entire class turned around to watch me. So I snuck a few glances from the corners of my eyes. I hadn't realized both Tony and Olivia were in this class. She sat down in the front while he was up in the nosebleed seats near me. I wished one or more of Tinfoil Hat's other Psychics were there instead—Henry or even Lane could sense the Psychic energy I'd exerted. Without Horace to spot for me, no one in the room would notice if I ran out of steam before dragging Rob out into the open.

But Olivia's gaze tilted up at the area overhead and then back at me. She gave me a thumbs-up just as Rob's translucent tricorn hat emerged from the ceiling like that troublemaking cat in the Seuss book. His eyes looked cartoonishly wide, too, but more alarmed. I smiled, knowing I had him as I crooked one index finger in his general direction. He floated down, slowly and steadily.

"Listen, I want you to head back home and play Go Fish with Ed or something." I put my hands on my hips, trying to mimic the authority Mrs. Redford notoriously used. But I wasn't a mom or even a tiny bit Italian. I wished I had one of her wooden spoons to brandish, at least, for any sympathetic Psychic energy it'd lend. I'd have looked like even more of an oddball than usual, though.

"Aww, but I've got stuff to do here on campus." Rob pouted. I glared back. The giant yawn that tore its way out of my chest ruined the effect.

"Fine." I rubbed one hand down my face before looking back at him. "You don't have to go home, but you can't stay in lecture halls or classrooms while Professors are teaching and students are trying to learn. It's not my rule. Maybe go take that up with Headmistress Thurston."

"Already tried it." Rob shook his head. "She can't see ghosts. Not in her current state."

"Well, duh." I rolled my eyes. Snark would have to do when authoritative presence didn't. "You can make an appointment to talk to her when I'm there. Or, you know, that other medium you've been acquainted with for the last twenty-four years." I jerked a thumb over my shoulder to indicate Mrs. Redford.

"You know, for a medium, you sure have a super-sized attitude." Rob stuck out his tongue, peering over my shoulder at Delilah Redford. His shoulders shook. "Super-sized like your butt."

"Seriously? Picking on the diabetic?" I raised an eyebrow. "All you've got to say for yourself is a fast-food fat joke?" I shook my head. "From a three-hundred-year-old ghost, I expected some kind of Colonial quip, not sitcom laugh-track fodder like that."

"He called you super-sized, didn't he?" Tony Gitano hissed in Rob's general direction. The cat shifter looked angrier than I'd have expected for a joke at my expense. "He's damn lucky Horace ain't here with Blaine's two dads."

"Oops." Rob tilted his hat at me. "I'm sorry for any insult. Tell the cat-man I apologized and I'll reconsider your request to leave."

I relayed his message to Tony and tapped my foot. Rob didn't move anything except his head. I understood he was looking around the room for any other ghosts. There weren't any. His lips curled into a sneer that might have made Elvis Presley jealous. I got tired of waiting.

"Done enough reconsideration?"

"Almost. But there's one more thing." Rob's smirk twisted like he was in pain. "Something important you should know about... hmm. How should I put this delicately? Ah. An old friend and mentor of yours."

"So say it already and stop taking up class time." With that sentiment, I sent along a hefty dollop of my Psychic energy, attempting to put Rob under a compulsion to vanish once he finished talking. I blinked when I sensed another Psychic's energy around the old ghost, pushing right back.

"You can't trust—" Rob's voice cut off with a screech that made the hair on the back of my neck stand up. "I can't. Sorry. Can't finish saying that."

Before I could check to see whose energy had pushed back at my compulsion attempt, Rob went from translucent to invisible, fading himself out of the lecture hall. He'd told nothing but the truth, even though it couldn't possibly be the whole truth.

I sank down into the nearest aisle seat, opened my satchel, and chewed on a Power Bar, the cookies and cream kind. Locking wills with Rob and who or whatever else had a hold on him had taken a lot out of me, and I couldn't afford to risk a hospital visit. I still had Professor Watkins' mysterious blue aura to research.

I stopped to grab more Power Bars at the dining hall before heading across to the library. All they had were the oatmeal kind, with and without raisins. Yucky, but they'd have to do in a pinch. The September night air was cool, but still warm enough for me to grab a cardigan instead of a jacket. I watched people, both the embodied and otherwise, file down Thayer Street on their way to wherever or whoever was important to them at that hour of the evening.

I leaned against the wall between the library doors and the bench, taking out my phone to call my mom. She wasn't too thrilled that I'd kept the job at Providence Paranormal, a decision that had saved us loads in tuition and fees. The downside, however, was that it would take twice as long to graduate. It also meant I stayed on the campus year-round, even over the summer. I missed her, but not Chepachet. I'd grown up in that tiny town, chosen so my family could hide the fact that they were Psychics. Even after the Reveal and the way the laws had been exceptionally easy on our kind, some of the older generation weren't comfortable with being out about it.

"Bianca!" The high-pitched squeal in Mom's voice evoked instant guilt. I had no idea how much time had passed since I'd last called. And she wasn't the type of mother to nag about it, either.

"Hi, Mom." I smiled, not because I felt like it, but so the expression would come through in my voice. I always wanted Mom to think I was happy, healthy, taking care of myself. Especially because most of the time, I wasn't and didn't. "How are you?"

"Amazing now. It's so good to hear from you, sweetheart!" I heard a click as she put me on speaker. "Are you taking a study break?"

"Almost done with one. Just about to study some more, actually." I reached into my satchel, grabbing a packet of raisins. My smile had faltered, and I didn't want to take the chance that my blood sugar was to blame instead of concern for everyone involved in all the Extramagus madness. Didn't want to make Mom worried, either.

"You work so hard, Bianca." I heard a series of ceramic clinks, which meant Mom was putting the dishes away. I closed my eyes, imagining the earthenware sailing through the air on the wings of Mom's Telekinesis and settling in place. "Remember to have fun while you're at school, as well."

"I do, Mom."

"Well, you haven't told me much about your classmates lately." A quiet, good-natured chuckle acted as a prelude to her next question. "How's that girl? What was her name again, Cassandra?" I heard her snap her fingers three times, something she always did when trying to remember something. "You know. The Precog gal with the Psychic weather app."

"Oh!" I sighed, shook my head. "You know, I'm not sure where Cassandra went. Haven't heard from her since the end of fall semester last year."

"Well, you should look her up sometime." The clinks turned to clatters as Mom moved on from plates to spoons and forks. "Your ghost friend, Horace, is pretty good about reminding you to eat, but he's not exactly the kind of buddy you bring to a restaurant. How long has it been since you went to East Side Pockets for falafel and baklava?"

"Way too long, Mom." I opened my eyes, staring out at the empty library steps, then looked up at the big, cloudless, light-polluted sky. This night's balmy weather was a far cry from the four feet of snow we'd gotten just before exams last December, which was the last time I'd seen Cassandra. "Psychic weather app…" I almost dropped the phone, but all of a sudden, Horace was there. He caught my fingers, pressing them against the glass and plastic. "Mom, my study buddies are here. I've got to go hit the books. I love you."

"Love you too, sweetie."

I waited until Mom hung up like I always did. Then, I tapped the icon for the LORA app that Kimiko Ichiro had installed everyone's phones over the summer in Newport. "LORA, do a correlation search for Psychic weather apps, the snowstorm last year, and the name Cassandra Spanos."

"Correlating. Shall I draw connections to the previously completed conclusions?"

"Yeah, that'd be great. Thanks, LORA." I pushed on the library door before remembering I had to pull. Ghosts had it easy in that regard.

"Thank you for participating in this conclusion-drawing activity." LORA's programmed voice response made me chuckle. I tucked the phone away in my pocket before heading inside.

The tables near the library lobby stood empty and at first I floundered, wondering where everyone else was. I waved to the helper ghosts hovering around the computer and card catalog. Back in January, I'd convinced them to come back to the library after it had a hole torn in it when a Grim attacked vampires on campus. I stopped, standing there and just watching them for a few moments.

That was why I'd almost forgotten about Cassandra, her potentially coincidental weather app, and her long absence. All the destruction and death. Ever since exam week last December, the ghosts were on edge, and I couldn't blame them. Most of the living people on campus didn't think the ice falling on Lynn Frampton's head was anything but an accident. The ghosts knew better.

Some of them, especially the ones who'd been Precognitive while alive, could tell when people risked dying. They got downright antsy when that happened. The helper ghosts had gone nuts during Intersession when two vampires had their fangs harvested, and their unlives ended. It had been just as bad right before Spring Break when Wilfred got killed. In fact, a few of the Psychic ghosts hadn't renewed their contracts with the school, opting for placement elsewhere instead.

Rob behaved completely opposite during all of that. He was one of the Redford family ghosts, so he was more concerned with them than the school in general. He'd popped in occasionally once Fred started courses at PPC, but Rob had been hanging around more frequently since fall semester started. Rob had to be worried about some kind of mortal danger here at the college, someone important to him or Fred. Tonight he should have been home, protecting Ed, who'd been abducted by Seelies at the beginning of the summer.

Just as I was about to leave the library and pay the Redford home a visit, Horace popped his head out of a bookshelf and beckoned. I rolled my eyes when he vanished through the stacks again, even though I knew where he'd gone. My woolgathering would have to wait. It might bear more fruit once LORA had some results, anyway.

CHAPTER SEVEN

Horace

Usually, when I stuck my head out of something solid, Bianca laughed. She barely cracked a smile this time. I wondered what my partner was thinking but, as usual, couldn't know. I'd given up asking about a year ago, the last time I'd changed the subject when she wanted to discuss Possession. She was ready, but I wasn't. Avoiding the hanging topic felt like navigating a room crowded with elephants no one would look at. I stuck my head back through the bookcase again, pulling a funny face this time.

"Who's over there?" Bianca's voice was flatter than a week-old soda.

"Tony and Kim." I let my features go back to resting ghost face. "Olivia. Henry Baxter. That new dragon librarian."

"You mean Mr. Waban?" She lifted her gaze off the floor.

"Yeah. The double dragon dad ghosts are there, too." I sighed. "Don't worry, I already made them promise not to argue."

"Good." Bianca turned the corner, then walked past the windowed closet that used to be a phone booth before everyone and their grandma had a smartphone.

The old ghost who lived in there gave Bianca a once-over then dropped me a wink. I nodded instead of rolling my eyes as usual. He had a point. When everyone else thought your relationship was romantic instead of platonic, it might be time to man up, confess, and let the lady decide how it was going to be from then on. My train of thought from before teetered its way back onto the rails. I'd have to tell Bianca how I felt and why it scared me at some point, and soon. But that night we had too much work to do.

"I have the books you requested, Miss Brighton." Mr. Waban, the ice dragon librarian, set a small stack of hardback books with threadbare canvas covers down at the unoccupied end of the table. Over on the other side, Tony and Kimiko hovered around the coded letter. The memory Psychic and vampire, Henry Baxter, sat in front of a skinny, rectangular, metal lockbox. He handed an old, chewed pencil to Olivia, who put a checkmark in a notebook with a red pen, then set the pencil inside a shoebox.

"LORA, note that I erased a memory of Richard Hopewell's from back when we were twelve. He used magic to cheat on an exam in eighth grade, but never told me what kind or how." Henry sighed and shook his head, then used a stylus to shut off the app's voice capability. "I can't figure out why I kept helping him."

"Why do any of us help each other?" Bianca sat down in front of the small pile of books and grabbed the one on top.

"Because coincidence threw us all into this together, probably." Olivia didn't look up from her notebook. "Would take a team of master Magi months to find out for sure, though. The silver dollar's next on this list, Henry."

"Ugh." Henry rubbed his eyes. "I need some air first, I think."

"You mean a cigarette?" Tony looked up from the codebreaking, his grin reminding me of the cat who hadn't quite eaten the canary yet but knew the cage stood open.

"Those will kill you, cat-man." Kimiko clucked her tongue

against her teeth. "Blaine will be upset. Says he's got dibs." She blew a raspberry.

"Hey, cats are supposed to have nine lives, right?" Tony shrugged, then slid his chair back and stood up. "I don't smoke, anyway, but we need a break. Gonna get a coffee or whatever instead."

"Here, got something for you." I hadn't even seen Olivia's hand go in her bag, but she stopped Tony in his tracks with the thermos she held up. "It's hot and light, only a little bit sweet."

"Really?" Tony blinked. "You don't want it?"

"Don't need as much coffee as I used to." Olivia let go of the thermos, and even though Tony didn't touch it, it landed on his upturned palm.

"Okay," Tony mumbled. He stalked after his vampire friend, holding the beverage.

Bianca watched them leave, then turned to look at Olivia. "Doesn't it ever bother you?"

"What?"

"That he never thanks you for anything?"

"He can't. I'm not the kind of legal eagle who'd get on his dad's payroll." The owl shifter opened a battered and dog-eared paperback, holding it up over her face as she read. Olivia Adler sure knew how to make an exit without moving an inch. "I'm the enemy as far as Gino Gitano's concerned."

"Um, Bianca?" I hovered in front of her, completely aware that half of me was under the table. I looked like I wore a wooden tutu. That was the whole point, of course.

"Hmm?" She turned past the flyleaf on her book and ran one finger down the Table of Contents. She glanced up and froze.

"Thank you." I bowed at the waist, making a little flourish with one hand. "For everything." I winked.

Her laughter rang out but stopped at the stacks, muffled by all the books. I couldn't feel the incorporeal corners of my mouth turn up, but I remembered the sensation of my long-gone body smiling as I watched and listened to her mirth. Once she'd caught her breath, Bianca explained for the peanut gallery. Off to my right, Kimiko giggled. Olivia's book jiggled a bit. A puff of something way too cold to be smoke misted out from behind Bianca's head, forming a pale-gray nimbus around her lavender hair.

I watched Mr. Waban stifling his laughter and decided he wasn't so bad, stuffy old dragon or not. But just as I'd figured that maybe the old fellow could redeem my opinion of his entire category of shifters, Willie and Iggy showed up.

"We promised not to argue, and that's exactly what we'll do." Wilfred's finger was in Ignacius Harcourt's face.

"Word crime!" Ignacius snorted. "You just implied we'd fight, airhead! Can't believe Hertha married a dumb blond like you."

"Shh!" Wilfred Harcourt pointed at me. "He's here. Stop."

Ignacius folded his arms over his chest, stopping short of the table I stood in the middle of. Wilfred pushed through to join me.

"Hmm." Bianca gazed at Wilfred, then glanced at Ignacius. "Interesting."

"I beg your pardon?" Wilfred raised an eyebrow.

"Oh, it's just unusual for the newer ghosts to pass through solid objects so easily." Bianca shrugged. "Usually, doing something like that means you've been incorporeal for at least a decade or two. And it's just been since March for you. You're pretty strong for a newbie. Congratulations."

"Ah." Mr. Waban's head moved in a slow nod. "Hello, Wilfred."

I turned my head, watching the air dragon's ghost narrow his eyes at the librarian. Beyond his translucent profile, I saw Kimiko wipe tears off her face, smearing mascara to make dark circles under her eyes. I'd almost forgotten she'd been standing right there when Blaine's stepdad had died. Been murdered, actually.

Olivia patted her shoulder absently, staring off in Wilfred's direction above her paperback. I tried to catch the owl shifter's eye, still wondering whether she could actually see us ghosts. She shouldn't be able to. Her eyes were naturally amber-colored and hadn't gone all owlish. I'd seen Olivia Adler enough times to know that she looked unusual for a nonmagical shifter. The magical ones carried attributes of their shifted forms while human, like Blaine's smoke rings and Kimiko's striped hair. Olivia's coloring marked her as more than mundane.

But Olivia Adler didn't look like a garden-variety owl shifter, or act like one, either. All the naturally occurring magical types except Tanuki and Dragons had vanished. But this was the third time I thought I'd caught her looking at incorporeal people, and I wasn't going to stand for it.

"Bianca, you really ought to ask her how she can see me." I locked gazes with my medium, then jerked my chin at Olivia.

Bianca waved a hand between Wilfred and Olivia. "So, how long have you been able to see ghosts while unshifted?"

"Um." Olivia blinked. Her hand dropped from Kimiko's shoulder, which was just as well since the Tanuki sprang from her seat as though the poor owl shifter was radioactive or something. "Hoo, boy." Olivia put the book down. "It's been on and off since I stopped taking all the meds that made me diurnal. My mom thinks it's some kind of weird side effect that'll go away eventually."

"And you didn't bother telling us you could see ghosts before now, why?" Kimiko put her hands on her hips.

"I never knew I could in human form." Olivia's gaze dropped to the table. "And like I said, it's probably some temporary fluke, anyway."

"I find that hard to believe." I watched Kimiko's face as she spoke, so I saw what Olivia missed. The Tanuki wasn't angry or even snarky. She looked almost excited, like an explorer discovering uncharted territory.

"Believe it, or you don't get my help on this anymore." Tony slapped one hand down on top of the encoded letter. I hadn't even noticed he'd returned.

"But don't you think it seems impossible for her not to know something like that?" Kimiko tapped one foot after another against the parquet floor, bouncing slightly. "She must have some idea. It's so mysterious. I mean, who puts small children on medication for their whole entire lives, anyway? People hiding something that's who. I wonder if LORA can figure it out."

The chair squeaked as it dragged against the floor and the flip-flops on Olivia's feet flapped on the wood like wings against air, carrying her away. Kimiko's hands went to her mouth, and Bianca's jaw dropped. Tony dashed after her but came back a few moments later.

"She took off. Literally." He sank back into the chair he'd occupied before. "I will too unless you promise to—"

"Apologize?" Kimiko nodded and sat back down. "Yeah, I went off like an insensitive mystery-solving nerd. I screwed up. Absolutely. And to you, too, Tony. I should have listened and dropped it. Sorry."

"Forgiven on my end." Tony leaned over the table again, peering at the yellowed paper. "If only your mate swallowed pride like you, the pack would be way better off."

Kimiko was once bitten, twice shy. She bypassed that line of conversation so far she might as well have detoured through the Under. Instead, she doodled on the blank notebook page next to her and muttered something about cyphertext.

"I'm not going to bother asking where Olivia went." Henry sat back down in front of the box, eying the notebook the owl shifter had left behind. "I need to keep on checking these memory charms. For great justice."

"Yeah." Tony leaned one hand against his cheek, leaning forward to peer at the paper again. "Until all their data belongs to us."

"Well, what can the ghosts and I do to help?" Bianca stretched in her seat.

"Ghosts, plural?" Henry glanced around. "You mean, besides the library helper ghosts?"

GHOST OF A CHANCE

"Yeah." Bianca nodded at me. "Horace is here, of course, but also Wilfred and Ignacius."

"Wilfred?" Henry raised an eyebrow. "Mr. Harcourt?" Henry stood up and straightened the leather jacket he always wore. "Hello, sir. I didn't mean to be rude, but I had no idea you were here."

"Please, tell him to forget about all those old pre-Reveal formalities." Wilfred sighed, drawing one weary hand down and slightly through his face. "And let him know that any friend of Blaine's is a friend of mine."

Bianca relayed the message, and Henry sat down, a faint yet relieved grin on his face. I had to stop myself from floating up through the table as my pride for her inflated like a helium balloon. She didn't muddle anything important or try to frame it according to her own speech patterns and perspective. Other Mediums, even on occasion the experienced and important ones like Delilah Redford, did.

Bianca was nothing fancy in solid terms, just plain according to them in so many ways even, with the changing hair color. But it suited her spirit, I thought. To me, she was like water—authentic, original, crystal clear, and the first thing anyone crossing a desert thinks of. I glanced at the dragon ghosts, closed my eyes for a moment, and considered my situation.

Ghosts were all in a perpetual state of passage, halfway between where we'd been and where we still had to go. The world needed more mediums like Bianca Brighton. More mundane solids like her, too. The first question she asked most people was "How can I help?" I wasn't sure I deserved to be her partner. Only she could decide whether and how she wanted me in her life.

A thud slammed the door on those thoughts, heavily. Henry Baxter fell to the floor. His arms and legs flailed, heavy boots striking hardwood, the fallen chair, and the nearest table leg.

"LORA, call Maddie." Tony's voice rang through the library at a volume most wouldn't risk with a dragon librarian present. "Lynn too."

Tony narrowed his eyes, but not before I saw them go catlike. He pounced on Henry, leveraging his body weight to keep the vampire from breaking himself or anything else. All I could think about was the wooden furniture everywhere and how a broken chair could stake him or something. My death energy sense was tingling. Someone in this room would risk death in the not-too-distant future. Maybe even more than one of them.

Somehow, Tony's shoulders seemed more bulky, indicating some sort of partial shift. That should have been impossible for a natural cat shifter like Tony Gitano. Only the magical shifters could partly shift anything but their eyes without a magipsychic charm. Maybe it was just the fact that he still wore his trench coat. For all I knew, he had such devices in the shoulder pads or something.

"What do we do?" Kimiko's face had gone pale.

"Get what's affecting him." Bianca tilted her head and stood on her toes, trying to get a good look at Henry's hands.

"Left. It's small and in his hand," I said. Energy was coming off of the object through the vampire's flesh and bone, something no living Psychic could see. Even Clairvoyants needed the right line of sight.

Tony threw his body across Henry's, holding on to his left wrist, so his fist stood raised, as though it held an invisible Excalibur out of a pond or something. And Taki Waban, dragon librarian, reached down to pry open the vampire's stronger-than-human fingers. Bianca slipped a particolored mitten onto one of her hands and scooped the small, transparent object from his palm.

"Is he okay?" Bianca blinked down at Henry, who'd stopped moving altogether. I thought he looked most sincerely dead.

"Gimme that bag, Maddie." Lynn Frampton slid on her knees past the dragon librarian and the cat-man like she'd been a softball all-star instead of Valedictorian. I didn't know her that well; maybe she'd been both. She stopped beside Henry, then reached one hand up and behind her toward her roommate. Maddie May tossed the plastic bag filled with ruby liquid underhand. Lynn caught it and shoved it in Henry's mouth.

"Drink!" Tony pulled one fist back, then slammed it into Henry's chest. "You can't conk out on us now!"

I understood what was going on. Lynn's coursework meant she knew, too. And Tony must have either been minoring in some medical stuff or doing an additional directed study on undead creatures. Vampires, especially Psychic or magically-empowered ones, could go into a deep sleep if something drained enough of their energy. It'd last for years if something didn't wake them up. Blood was one of those things, but cold, bagged blood like the girls had brought wouldn't do the trick without help. There was something else.

"Tell them to let Maddie try waking him." I'd watched the pair of them get together. Half their courtship had taken place on campus, after all.

"That's right! Maddie, get him awake and drinking." Bianca waved a page of notes from the Extrahuman Regulations class she and Olivia had been taking together. "You're one of three things that can wake a slumbering vampire, and the other two aren't exactly legal."

Tony got out of the way. Everyone looked on as Maddie's dusky hand closed over Henry's pale one. I made myself watch as she leaned down to murmur in his ear. I'd seen many such displays of affection in the years since I'd died, but it wasn't within the scope of my living experience. No one had ever touched or spoken to me with anything like that kind of affection during either my solid or incorporeal time, and none ever would if I couldn't ghost up and tell Bianca how I felt.

But the situation had gone from busy to life-threatening in under sixty minutes. It still wasn't time.

CHAPTER EIGHT

Bianca

"Quartz." I held the crystal up to the light, peering at it. "Infused with a whole lot of power, too." I screwed a magipsychic viewing monocle against my eye. The loaner device from Headmistress Thurston gave me limited ability to see the Magical energy I normally couldn't. I had no idea what type it was, only that it was there. "Only a little of it is Psychic, but it doesn't match yours, Henry. So, who's the Magus this belonged to, then?"

"Let me see?" Maddie held out her hand tentatively, like she approached a skittish horse and not a friendly but tired class-mate. I handed it over, mitten and all. She peered at it, shrugged, and passed it back. After that, she wiped her hand on her skirt, barely aware she did it. "Eww, I don't like that type of magic. It feels like a black hole. Who could this have belonged to?"

"Neil." Henry shook his head. "Not Fred's dad, Neil. One of my old friends. He had this with him every day at the hospital back in the days after I got turned."

"Hospital?" Lynn crossed her arms over her chest and raised an eyebrow. "Magi went to regular hospitals in the 1990s, during the worst parts of the Reveal? Wasn't that frowned on by the Magus community back then?"

"Neil had to." Henry sighed, relaxing his shoulders as Maddie rubbed them. "He had leukemia. I had no idea Neil had stored any of his memories, which is a good thing."

"Wait, what?" Tony's eyebrows almost collided. "You had a seizure and almost went dark on us, and you say it's a good thing?"

"Well, it means a different Psychic helped Neil put that memory in the crystal." Henry sighed again.

"Are you sure?" Maddie leaned her head against his, her curls cascading around them both. "Last time you didn't remember putting a memory somewhere, it was because you wiped it from your own mind at the time."

"I'm sure this time. The memory in this crystal didn't include a wipe. In fact, it didn't include me at all." Henry's mouth stretched in a grin that didn't bare his fangs. "That means Edgar must have helped Neil before he died. We're on the right track."

"So, what was in that memory crystal?" Lynn smirked. "Jeez, that could have come straight out of a *Stargate* episode. I feel like a bigger geek than usual."

"Neil was saying something, but I didn't get to find out what." Henry held his hand out.

"The jolt you got was magic, though." Maddie tapped her chin with one finger. "I saw it but didn't recognize the type. I knew it was there but couldn't see it. I've never even heard of a magic type that looks and feels like that."

"It must have been Neil's, then. He was a Null Magus." Henry rubbed his head. "I bet that was a ward against anyone but Edgar getting the memory out, but maybe the ward's broken after all that. I'll try it again." Henry stuck one hand out, palm up.

"Not here and not now." I closed my hand over the crystal. "Am I right, Lynn?"

"Absolutely." Lynn jerked her chin at the librarian. "If Mr.

Waban hadn't been here, we might not have gotten this magipsychic whosiwhatsis away from Henry in time. Next time Henry tries this, we need to make serious preparations."

"With what?" Tony rubbed his arms through the trench coat. "A young priest, an old priest, and some holy water?"

"Bagged blood, warmed, at least six pints." Lynn ticked off each item on a finger. "A bear-level or stronger shifter. Our pack Alpha. Someone in law enforcement, plus Mr. Ichiro. More than one powerful Magus with amplification devices or wands. It wouldn't hurt if one of those Magi was Headmistress Thurston. An actual non-student doctor, if one's willing to help a vampire try the psychometric version of extreme sports. Maybe Doctor Klein from the hospital would help. She's a vampire, too."

"I'm in agreement with Miss Frampton's ideas." Mr. Waban looked at me for some reason. "You seemed to know what was wrong immediately, Miss Brighton. You ought to be there again as well and bring whichever ghost helped you see it."

"Um, this is all fine and well, but Henry's thing is going to take time." Kimiko rattled the paper with the cipher on it. "And maybe we don't need to do something that risky, anyway. Because I think I figured something out here."

"Really?" Tony blinked, then smirked. "Without me?"

"With what you did already." Kim shrugged. "Anyway, I found two repeating patterns that look like names."

"Well, don't leave us hanging." Tony leaned on the table, trying to get a good look at the paper. His eyes moved from side to side. "Great balls of yarn! It says Edgar."

"Seriously?" Henry shook his head, his chuckle darker than his hair. "Coincidence is on the prowl tonight, huh?"

"Oh no, someone said the C-word." The voice from the doorway belonged to the green-haired man standing just inside it. "Let's go study somewhere else, Margot."

"Um, no." A redheaded woman ducked under the man's arm and sauntered into the room with the rest of us. She took one look at the overturned chair and moved to right it. "These guys helped us over the summer, Lane. We'll stay."

"Says the chick who came here to get her Ph.D." Lane Meyer shook his head. "I'm the C-average student who actually needs to study, you know." Even with the complaints, he sat down and started pulling books from his bag.

"So." I looked from Kimiko to Tony and back. "What's the other name there?"

"Joyce." Kimiko wrinkled her nose, then tapped her temple with one finger. "Familiar name; wait a second." She mimed putting a hat on, then pretended to turn a crank on the side of it. I tried not to get too distracted by the three wise ghosts laughing at her antics.

"Joyce was Edgar's lady." Henry's eyes got a faraway look. "Maybe they were married; I don't remember much about her, but she was always there when I went over for lessons with Edgar as a kid. Joyce made an amazing bologna sandwich, and an even better fluffernutter." Everyone but Margot gave Henry a sideways glance. "What? I was a kid in 1970s Rhode Island, okay? Anyway, she was also Precognitive."

"Woah, nice combo." Horace nodded his head, talking like the others could actually hear him. It was a habit he'd started picking up over spring semester around the Tinfoil Hat folks. "They could see just about anything coming and deal with it by making people forget everything."

"Ooh! Now I know where I remember the name Joyce from." Kimiko clapped her hands. "She was the Psychic who witnessed my betrothal." She tried explaining a complicated arranged marriage custom for dragon shifters, but I couldn't follow it except for the part where the kids had got checked by a Precognitive Psychic to see how powerful their offspring would be.

"Well, if this paper has something to do with Edgar and Joyce, it might help Professor Watkins." Olivia leaned in the doorway, gazing at the last empty seat next to me. "I think everyone knows this, but Edgar's his brother."

"Glad you're back, Olivia." I gestured at the seat. "Maybe we can fill you in on what happened earlier. Speaking of the professor, I have to look in these books to find out what that weird blue light around him was. It might be the reason he can't get back into his body."

"Woah, that's no ordinary coma! Watkins has been locked out of his body all this time?" Lynn snagged a chair from another table and crammed it near mine at a weird angle. "Let me help. He's only the best teacher in of the history of the known universe."

"Okay." I handed her half the books from the stack in front of me. She reached out and took two more.

"I speed-read." Lynn winked. I remembered how she'd solved Bobby's hibernation problem in only a few days.

"You rule." I smiled, then bent my head over the book I'd cracked earlier.

"I rule more." Horace stuck his hand through the book in line after my current one. His eyes went white.

"Creepazoid." I shook my head, then looked back down at the book. "Gross, Horace." After that I stuck my tongue out, so he'd know I didn't actually think he was gross.

"You talking about a wibbly-wobbly ghosty-wosty thing?" Lynn didn't even look up from her reading to ask.

"Talking to him about one, yeah." I wrinkled my nose. "Horace thinks he can read faster than you by some kind of incorporeal osmosis."

"Oh, no, he didn't." Lynn's eyes moved faster. Her fingers turned pages so quickly I wondered whether she had calluses like a guitar player's, except caused by paper cuts instead of metal strings.

Horace didn't bother with trash talk. Maybe he couldn't. His white-out eyes had gray streaks. At least, that's what I thought at first. I realized they were words, lines of text.

Not wanting to get left behind, I flipped to the table of contents of the book in my hands. It wasn't a dry research tome or even an old textbook. Instead, it was a series of curious cases presented in engaging prose.

"Try this one." The slender finger pressed against the page left behind a frosty print. I looked up into the creased brown face of Mr. Waban.

"Really?" I blinked, then glanced back down at the chapter title and read it aloud. *"The Curious Case of the Sleeping Beauty?"*

"Yes." He nodded. "Professor Watkins told me he'd found it most instructive during his undergraduate studies."

I pictured Nathaniel Watkins as a young student in this very library. But dragons like Taki Waban hadn't even been able to set foot on the PPC campus back in those days, so Nate Watkins must have borrowed it from the ice dragon's personal collection at that time. I didn't have time for further flights of fancy, or to ask Horace whether my mental image was correct. Instead, I turned my attention to the tale.

It wasn't much different from a traditional fairy tale as far as the plot went. Slighted Godmother, decade-plus vendetta, magical spindle. The differences were in the details. My eyes went wider than those of a kid walking into her surprise birthday party.

"Guys, I think the professor's problem is a soul spindle." I could barely believe I'd gotten the answer already, even before the brainiac. Had coincidence struck thrice in one night?

"What's a soul spindle?" Again, Lynn didn't look up. Her right hand scrawled notes on a sheet of paper beside her.

"It's an amalgamated magipsychic device that keeps Astral Psychics from leaving their bodies." Maddie peered over my shoulder. "I read about them last semester, but there's not much in Magus coursework about them because while we can help make them, we can't use them."

"But why would a device meant to keep a Psychic in his body make trouble for a dude who's been knocked out of it like Professor Watkins?" Everyone blinked as the Dean's Listers wrestled with the fact that Lane Meyer, C student, had asked the million-dollar question. I silently cheered the green-haired academic underdog.

"Because someone activated one on his body after he left it." Horace's eyes were still all white when he gave me the answer. I repeated his theory.

"Who'd do a thing like that?" Kimiko looked disgusted, with good reason. Her face mirrored how I felt about the whole idea. "I can't even or odd right now."

"Hairballs like Richard Hopewell, that's who." Tony folded his hands together, the pop of knuckles cracking reminding me of gunshots. "He'd better damn well hope that I never get my claws on him."

"He's definitely a hairball or worse, but he's still just a souped-up Magus," Margot said. "They can't use a magipsychic device for Psychic purposes."

"So, he had a Psychic's help at some point while Professor Watkins was unconscious last spring." Kimiko rubbed her upper arms like she was trying to get warm. "That'd be back during the fancy-dress ball last semester in Water Place Park. We already know he used mind magic to control Professor Brodsky last winter, so he could have whammied a vulnerable-enough Psychic while that creature attacked us."

"Allegedly mind-controlled Brodsky," Olivia corrected. "Well, I mean, we all know he did it, but that's how I have to talk about it until the trial. Anyway, there were definitely Psychics there. Elderly ones, maybe on medication. I'll call Jeannie and get a list." She got up and pulled out her phone, heading toward the not-exactly-empty old phone booth I'd passed on the way inside.

"Registration for soul spindles is a giant pain in the rear." Henry leaned back in his seat. "There hasn't been one on the books for maybe thirty years."

"That don't mean nothing." Tony snorted. "You think there ain't a black market for devices like that? Now it's my turn to make a phone call." He headed off in a different direction than Olivia though the cat shifter took one long look over his shoulder as he went.

"Hey, I found something else here about soul spindles." Lynn looked up this time, meeting my eyes through Horace's translucent form. "And it's nothing nice."

"What is it?" I clutched the curious case book like it was a lifeline and I was drowning in the Bay.

"If Professor Watkins got hit by that soul spindle whammy at the Water Place Park event, we're running out of time. If we don't get him back in his body by the end of the month, he'll never get back in."

"Okay, so how do we do that? Get him back in his body, I mean." Lane leaned on his elbows and peered at Lynn, but she shook her head.

"We don't. But there are three ways for someone else to do it." Lynn tapped a line she'd scribbled on the notebook. "The Psychic who activated it could voluntarily deactivate the spindle or cancel it by dying, but that's not likely. Plan B is, his destined love could break the thing's hold on him."

"No way he's got one of those." Margot shook her head. "Nate Watkins isn't the type."

"Anyone can fall in love." Kimiko shook her head. "Why not him?"

"Hmm, no. Not really. Nate Watkins is a confirmed bachelor. He's disinterested in romance of any sort." Mr. Waban closed his eyes and snapped his fingers a few times. "Your generation uses the terms a-romantic and asexual if I'm not mistaken?"

"Yeah, they're the A in LGBTQIA." Lane nodded. "So it

wouldn't matter if someone else loves him all unrequited-like. Coincidence doesn't let true love play on a one-way street."

"Well, scratch Plan B, then. The other way is for a powerful-enough incorporeal to tie themselves to the soul spindle." Lynn closed her eyes. "That might push his energy out of the thing and let him get back in his body."

"Finally!" Horace clapped his hands but only I heard it. "Something I can do! Ask that brainiac how, Bianca. I bet it's easy-peasy lemon-squeezy."

I asked. Lynn shut her eyes, and her lips pressed into a thin, flat line. It got silent, even for a library. After almost half a minute, she spoke.

"Ghosts don't get attached to soul spindles. Well, they do, technically, but they turn into wraiths and then the spindle tears them apart." Lynn looked at the stack of books Horace had been perusing. I guessed she was trying to catch his eye. "We need another Astral Projection Psychic still in their body. One of those could use it on themselves. That'd knock the professor out of its clutches."

"So, let's find ourselves a Projection Psychic, then." Kimiko smiled, then turned toward her tablet. "LORA, compile a list of Psychics who do astral projection within a hundred-mile radius of Providence."

But projection psychics were rare. It took LORA a week to come up with nothing within a hundred miles, nothing within five hundred, and nothing within a thousand. By then, it was too late.

CHAPTER NINE

Horace

I floated down the street behind Bianca, Lynn, and Blaine Harcourt. I wasn't exactly sure why the dragon shifter had insisted on tagging along, but it meant I had to endure hanging around with his two dads yet again. At least they kept their traps shut most of the way this time.

"So, her last name is Spanos." Blaine had both his hands in his jacket pockets. "Interesting."

"Ew." Lynn wrinkled her nose. "What are you going to bribe me with, Trogdor? You know, so I don't tell Kimiko you came with us just to check in on an old lady friend." Lynn's smirk might have seemed mean-spirited instead of sarcastic if she hadn't dropped Blaine a wink at the same time.

"I'm just connecting dots here, not revisiting an old love connection, which she wasn't by the way." A thin trail of smoke wafted out behind Blaine. "Spanos is Greek, and it means hairless."

"Well, she's not." Bianca shook her head. "Hairless, that is.

Cassandra's definitely Greek, though. Her grandparents immigrated back in the day."

"I wasn't thinking along literal lines." The smoke ring Blaine blew pulled into a long oval shape as it went past my left ear.

"Me neither." Lynn sighed. "I only met Cassandra one time, at the Homecoming Festival last year. She's the person who gave me this Psychic weather app." The human girl tapped her phone, then passed it to Bianca. Blaine pouted. "You've already seen it, dragon man."

"Anyway," Blaine went on, "in ancient Etruscan cultures, oracles shaved their heads so they could reduce interference on their connection to the Fates or whatever other powers that be they turned to. So, my bet is that the Spanos family has had their Psychic ability from ancient days."

"Why is that important?" Lynn shrugged. "Either Cassandra will be at home or not."

"Well, it means that maybe she's got a family member who knows more. Maybe even one who can find us an Astral Projection Psychic. And if she's gone missing, perhaps someone in her family will want to help us with our Extramagus problem."

"The boy gets his brains from me." Ignacius' voice rumbled behind me.

"His mother, you mean." Wilfred snorted. "And I'm the one who taught him all those good study habits."

"Quit it, or I'll make wraith-meat out of the both of you." I held up a fist. Silence reigned behind me.

"Or maybe not." Bianca shook her head, possibly to empty her ears of ghostly dragon arguments so she could focus on corporeal dragon ideas. "I remember when she started working on this app. A year before you started here, Lynn."

"How's that?" Lynn took the phone back from Bianca.

"That app is more Precognitive than anything else, but the weather detection has a thread of some other energy." Bianca shivered, pulling her jacket tighter around her.

"Yeah." Blaine nodded. "It had some Air and Water Magic if I remember correctly."

"What if that came from Richard Hopewell?" Bianca shook her head. "If he's got Cassandra somewhere, then her family might not be able to help us without risking her safety."

"Let me see that again." Blaine reached for the phone, and Lynn handed it over. "Oh, yeah, definitely magic. Three threads, actually: Water, Air, and Ice. The same magic energy types as in the storms last winter, Lynn. But I have no way of knowing who the magic came from. I won't jump to conclusions about it because all three of those elemental types are in the PPC faculty and the student body. You need to bring this to a magic CSI lab to figure that out."

"Look, here we are." Bianca pointed at the weathered shingle sided building, peering up at its eaves and gables. The Spanos house was over near Gano Street, in a recently trendy neighborhood. There were ghosts everywhere, though. Lots of them came from a hundred or more years back. Some things can't be renovated, and the incorporeal population of a place was one of them.

Lots of people who don't know better think ghosts are static, that we're echoes of the people we were while solid. We don't have to be. Corporeals are solid for a reason, even though us ghosts don't know what that is, and we're not like them after we die. We're fluid once we've shuffled off the mortal coil; malleable. We can look any way we want, change our clothes, our hair, or even our shapes on a whim, as long as we stay humanoid. All we have to do is free our minds. Like the song goes, the rest follows.

But as the other song goes, freedom is just another word for nothing left to lose. Some ghosts, especially the ones who stuck around under duress, commanded by opportunistic mediums for parlor tricks and financial gain, got a raw deal. Their contracts shackled them into a form of perpetually slavery most people couldn't see. The Reveal changed all that for us.

Laws and regulations hobbling Psychic and Magic practitioners set us free. Ghosts made only the contracts they wanted now, with required provisions for solids to stick to in the document. Psychic mediums could no longer lie about us moving on, so family members left us at their mercy. No more ordering us to make fake hauntings so they could turn a profit. We got to seek out what we hadn't been able to in life. If I wanted to run around looking like a Tolkien elf, I could do that. But all I wanted was my bowler hat and the long brown coat from a time long before my solid body had been born. And to help Bianca, always that.

"I wonder how they manage paying the taxes on this place." Blaine blew a few smoke rings. "All the property values went way up, but the house looks like it needs work that'd been put off."

"I think I know how they keep it." I pointed at a potted gardenia on the stoop by the side door. Along with the flowering plant was an herb.

"You guys?" Bianca nudged Lynn and jerked her chin at the flower pot. "What's in there besides the little red flowers?"

"That's catnip." Lynn wrinkled her nose.

"Well, what's it mean?" Leave it to Bianca to ask. She believed the old adage that there was no such thing as a stupid question.

"Gattos. The people in this house are theirs." Blaine's smoke lost its ring shapes, increasing in volume until I wondered whether his nose hairs had caught fire. "The Spanos family is either on the Gitano payroll or under their so-called protection. I am. Sick. To death. Of fracking cat-men."

"Oh, please. No need to get all Shatner when you talk." Lynn rolled her eyes and snatched her phone away from the angry dragon. "I know the shifter Mafia took potshots at you, Trogdor, but you really need to chill out and stop generalizing already."

"I need no such thing." Blaine put his hands on his hips. The two of them facing off reminded me of Lisa and Bart Simpson.

"Well, the rest of us do. For all the research we gotta get done, anyway." Lynn punched the dragon shifter in the shoulder. "We could have used your help last night, but you refused to even be in the same room as Tony. You're cramping our study time."

"Shh!" The hissed command came from a tiny rectangular window near the ground. I looked down to see a shock of gray hair, a forehead, and a pair of eyes peeking out from behind a dingy pane of glass.

"Huh?" Bianca kept her voice low.

"If you're friends with Tony, get lost."

"You don't understand." Lynn shook her head. "Tony's not like his dad's—"

"I do understand, and they'll end him if they think he's not loyal. They'll do the same to us. The bonds between our families are new." The head turned, and I noticed that the profile matched what I remembered of Cassandra's. This had to be an older relative of hers. "Go to the senior center. Talk to Donato. And don't come back, 'specially if you're gonna argue like that about the boy."

"But—" Lynn's protest got cut off by Blaine's hand over her mouth. She was the most book-smart person I'd ever seen, but her street smarts were chronically absent.

The dragon shifter nodded and turned around, Lynn and all. He walked back down the street the way we had come, Bianca trotting to catch up with them. I followed along with the pair of shocked dragon dads in tow.

The senior center was the last place any self-respecting ghost wanted to go. The death energy around places like that without the balance of healing and life present at places like hospitals makes us uneasy. But if Bianca had to be there, I'd deal with it. I glanced over my left shoulder, then my right. It seemed like Ignacius and Wilfred had similar sentiments about Blaine. I wouldn't be alone, at least.

Bianca

"I'll tell her you want to visit her." Donna Murphy, CNA, spun on her heel and then looked back over her shoulder. Her shiny brown bobbed hair bounced with authority. "She might say no, though. You know how it is with Psychics." The grin she wore made it clear that she considered the Senior Center's denizens part of her family.

I waited in the back parlor with Blaine and Lynn, the decor and furnishings reminding me of the Nocturnal Lounge even though sunlight streamed through the cream-colored lace draperies framing the windows. Lynn peered at the bookshelves while Blaine side-eyed a vase that was definitely not Ming Dynasty even though it made an attempt to be. Horace, Ignacius, and Wilfred hissed so many whispers at each other they might as well have been frying eggs on a griddle.

"What's going on?" I raised an eyebrow as I murmured, hoping none of the staff or seniors walking by in the hall would notice I spoke to what they'd think was thin air.

"Wilfred's saying we should be out looking for the spindle." Horace rolled his eyes.

"I tend to agree," Ignacius said. The other two blinked at him right along with me. The two former husbands of Hertha Harcourt had always been at odds before. "With the amount of energy something like that puts out, it should be easy to track."

"I'm trying to explain to double dragons here that we ghosts can't do anything about the spindle except sense it." Horace sighed. "If whoever has it can see us, they'll just move."

"Technically, that's not true." Wilfred narrowed his eyes at his old rival. "If we're willing to make a sacrifice, we could be out there taking the fight to Hopewell's Psychic friends."

"Friends?" Ignacius tilted his head exactly like Blaine was doing at the Monet print above the fireplace on the other side of the room. "Thought it was just one Psychic, and mind-controlled at that."

"It could be a medium, so technically there'd be a ghostly medium partnering with the solid. And mind magic only controls living people." Wilfred spoke through a clenched jaw. "You have a forty-year jump on me in the being dead department, plus five hundred years of life as a dragon, and you don't realize this?"

"And you don't realize you're accusing either Delilah Redford or her ten-year-old son here?" Ignacius wrung his hands. "They're both good people, and the only other mediums besides Bianca in Rhode Island, in case you forgot."

"Well, what about Henry's memory trinkets? Edgar wiped a lot of minds before the Reveal and the Registry. And Henry covered for Hopewell more than once." Wilfred's voice stayed even and calm despite his paranoid musings. "We've no idea how many mediums there are around here who are unregistered."

"Iggy's right, there are only three." Horace tapped the rim of his bowler hat. "I'm a ghostly medium. It doesn't matter who's in the Registry and who isn't. We can sense the solid mediums."

"Don't you need some kind of proximity for that?" Wilfred crossed his arms over his chest.

"You forget that Bianca and I recently went all over the state looking for Edgar Watkins." Horace shook his head. "Only three living mediums at that time, but there were more ghostly ones around. Which is a good thing."

"How so?" Wilfred seemed to relax a bit, though I could practically see the wheels turning in his head.

"Some other time." Horace jerked his chin at the doorway.

"Hello there." A birdlike lady with hair so white it was almost pink stepped into the room. She sauntered over to a settee and took to it with a flair that almost hid her slight limp from us. "I'm Mrs. Donato. I insist you three have a seat though Miss Brighton's other friends can do as they please since I can't see whether or not they sit in any event."

"She's insisted you have tea, too." Donna chuckled in counterpoint to the squeaky wheel on the tea cart she pushed into the room. I eyed it warily, remembering Jeannie La Montaigne's unluckiest day from last semester. She'd told me about the faulty tea cart incident. "Don't worry, the wheels have been cleared by the handyman since its tea spilling rampage this past spring."

Donna set a tray with a pot, sugar bowl, cream pitcher, and four cups with saucers on the table between the settee and the sofa. Lynn, Blaine, and I took seats. The dragon leaned on the right arm of the couch, peering out the window behind Mrs. Donato. His eyes shifted until he had vertical pupils, which meant he was monitoring her energy. Lynn took out one of her notebooks and a pencil, then settled in like this was a heavy study session instead of a friendly visit. I leaned forward and poured some tea for each of us.

"Thank you, Miss Brighton." Mrs. Donato's smile was as bright as a sunrise. She reached across and toppled a dollop of cream into her cup, then stirred with a clink of silver on china.

"So, we came here on advice from someone in a house over on—"

"Please, no direct questions or references to what brings you here today," said Mrs. Donato. She picked up her cup and blew across it, then gazed for a moment at the swirling steam. "I already knew I'd be giving a reading or three this afternoon. Preambles muddle my process."

"So, what do you want to talk about, then, Mrs. Donato?" Lynn tucked her pencil behind her ear.

"Jeannie and Ismail, of course," the elderly woman beamed. "Aren't they a lovely couple?"

"Oh yeah." Lynn shrugged with one shoulder. "I guess. I'm glad Jeannie found her mate because she's Bobby's cousin and all, but—"

"Oh, don't worry, dear." Mrs. Donato winked. "They won't upstage your wedding."

"Wait, my what?" Lynn blinked.

"Well, haven't I just about prattled my silly head off!" Mrs. Donato actually giggled. She sounded almost like a kid. I felt a surge of Psychic energy from her the moment before she spoke again. "What I mean about Jeannie and Ismail is, the two of them ought to be here in Providence."

"But they're not." Blaine turned his head, leveling his gaze at the frail woman as though she were as strong as he was. He may have been right, too, because he'd been checking her energy the whole time. "They're in the Under, visiting the Goblin King for some kind of Unseelie court function."

"Exactly." Mrs. Donato sipped her tea. "But they should be here, Ismail especially. In fact, they should return immediately."

"Bianca, you have to ask her why." Horace was so agitated I started shivering. Glancing to the side, I saw Lynn's breath as she dropped the notebook to curl her hands around the teacup in front of her. "There's death in the air."

I leaned forward, gazing into the older Psychic's eyes. "Why do they need to come back, Mrs. Donato?"

"So far, call it a hunch. But please," the elderly Psychic tilted her cup at the three of ours, "finish your tea, and I will tell you all you need to know.

Lynn gulped a few times, swirled, then gulped again. Blaine mumbled something about tea being for widows and dashed it down like a shot of tequila. I glanced down to find mine was already gone, so I set the cup back in its saucer and waited.

Mrs. Donato finished her beverage after we did ours. She set the cup down so gently it made no sound. Her head tilted to the left and then to the right as it bent over the table and all four cups. I hadn't noticed at first that she'd been holding her breath. When she exhaled, a surge of Psychic energy stronger than anything I'd felt from a living person pushed out from her in a surge. Not a pebble in a pond, a boulder.

"Oh, dearie me." Mrs. Donato didn't lean back, she sagged, and her eyes closed. Horace rushed to her side even though he couldn't do anything to help. Wilfred and Ignacius shot up toward the ceiling, stopping short of passing through. Blaine sneezed.

"I'm getting Donna." Lynn stood up, the notebook and pencil falling from her lap to the floor.

"No." The elder shook her head, her gaze glassy and distant. "Get Ismail. One of your friends will need him to contest something. And you." She pointed at me. "You'll spend some time alone soon." She tilted her eyes up and to her left, where Horace hovered. "More than one of your incorporeal friends faces a big decision. The Watkins brothers erred in judgment when both the dragons passed." She pointed at Blaine. "His father's death broke a heart and no one bothered to help heal it, and his mother made more mistakes. Neither brother stepped forward to mend them when they could have, and now they're stuck. The generation between yours and mine can't fix this. You've got to do better than your parents did when they faced similar troubles."

"But why do we need Ismail?" Blaine leaned forward, smoke trailing out of both his nostrils. He was angry, of course. I would be, too, if she'd singled out my parents. "If he can't come, we have to know so we can pick an Unseelie backup."

"It's unclear. But I see darkness, furred tails, pointed ears." Mrs. Donato yawned. "And you don't need a Djinn's magic or an Unseelie Faerie of rank. It's who he is that matters." She turned her eyes on Lynn, gave her a faded smile. "You can go and get Donna now, young healer. Your part in this chapter is done, but they'll need you again later on."

"Um, sure?" Lynn turned and trotted out of the room.

When the Nursing Assistant returned, she took one look at Mrs. Donato, then shooed us out with one hand and grabbed the phone on the wall with the other.

I walked down the hall with my two corporeal friends and

three less solid ones, listening to the sound of Lynn's pencil documenting everything we'd seen and heard.

Visiting Mrs. Donato had been a bit like consulting a magic eight ball. The outlook was cloudy. And things definitely got more confusing and dangerous before they came clear.

CHAPTER TEN

Horace

I lagged behind in the foyer, stopping Ignacius and Wilfred by sticking my hands out to either side of me. They halted, but the authoritative effect was ruined when a lady with a walker mumbled something Italian into an old flip phone and hobbled inside, walking straight through us.

"Shouldn't you be following her, Horace?" Ignacius jerked his chin at Bianca's retreating back. "She looks a little paler than usual."

"Yeah, you and I will." I nodded at Wilfred. "He won't."

"I— Um, what?" Wilfred didn't usually stammer, but I had caught him off guard, after all.

"You're going on a quest to find a Redford." I crossed my arms over my chest. "Or that insufferable Rob."

"But I thought splitting the party was a bad idea." Wilfred shook his head.

"We need a second set of Psychic eyes on this and Ignacius is right, Bianca does look pale." I started slowly out over the sidewalk. "Check the Redfords' house first, I'd prefer Ed's help over his mom's."

"Really? But she's way more experienced than a ten-year-old kid." Wilfred raised his eyebrow.

"Call it a hunch, but I think Ed might have information we need, and he's definitely on our side." I beckoned to Ignacius. "None of the solids have bothered talking to him since Fred's adventure to rescue him, but that doesn't mean we should follow their lead."

"Yeah, I understand." Wilfred nodded. "The living can be a bit dense. I sure was."

"Nice one, Willie." Ignacius chuckled.

"Thanks, Iggy."

I glanced over my shoulder, watching them float little golf waves at each other and snickered. If the double dragon dads could get along, maybe the Harcourt family fences had a chance of getting mended in the solid world as well someday.

Bianca

On the way back to campus from the Senior Center, my phone beeped. I tapped it to find a message from Olivia.

Jeannie's list of seniors invited to and actually at the charity ball.

I scrolled down, checking all the names. "Well, Mrs. Donato was there. But wait. Who is Katherine Rogers, and why was she on the guest list and not at the event?" I tapped the phone to bring up google and searched her name. I found an obituary for a month before the ball. She'd been ninety-one. I added the information to the list, then selected the Tinfoil Hat group and sent to all. No more splitting the party. We needed each other.

Blaine's stiff shoulders as he and Lynn argued made me worry. The first person he thought of from Mrs. Donato's description had been Nox Phillips, who turned into a big, black,

Unseelie horse with water magic. Lynn said it could have something to do with Josh Dennison's missing older brother Derek, who was a werewolf and had gone missing after getting in trouble with the law toward the end of the Reveal.

I felt in my gut that the prediction pointed to Tony and thought Blaine should know better. Ismail wasn't related to the Dennisons in any way. He'd had nothing to do with Nox's family, either. But the Djinn had paid a ton of attention to Tony since Jeannie brought his lamp to campus last spring. They even looked a bit alike, something around the eyes and the bridge of the nose. And that hunch of mine just wouldn't quit.

Trotting to catch up, I intended to explain. It was no use. Ghosts along the way kept interrupting me, trying to stop and talk, which made me sound spacier than I already felt. Blaine might as well have been wearing headphones for all the good my attempts at conversation did, and Lynn kept side-eyeing me. She handed me a squat bottle of water. I slowed down to twist the cap off and drink a bit. As the two most book-smart people I knew kept their pace, I heard Lynn snark at Blaine about reptiles lacking ears. I shuffled along, taking another swig of water, then grinning as I realized she was sticking up for my incoherently babbling self.

I yawned, suddenly exhausted from all the Psychic backlash at tea. And I wanted to stop walking but figured it'd be a bad idea for Blaine and Lynn to lose me. I wasn't sure whether anyone but the fellow in the basement had seen us leave the Spanos house and head to the senior center. Tangling with the Gatto Gang was the last thing I wanted to do. I drank the last of the water, then tossed the bottle into a green recycling bin.

Even though Lynn was shorter than me, she power-walked with a competitive vengeance so she could keep slightly ahead of Blaine as she good-naturedly told him off. I wouldn't have had a problem with keeping up if I hadn't been so fatigued. I tapped the phone again, which made me jealous. It got to go back to sleep. I was terminally tired, as usual. I wondered why Horace wasn't at my elbow, telling me to eat something.

The toe of my sneaker snagged on the sidewalk somehow. Okay, maybe it didn't. I'd tripped on nothing. The phone clattered to the pavement on its back, the case protecting it from shattering. I could be more than just exhausted. Had my medication alarm gone off while it was silenced at the Senior Center? Had I eaten breakfast? I couldn't remember. Slipping up when you have diabetes is like walking into quicksand.

I squinted, trying to focus on the PPC logo emblazoned across the back of Lynn's sweatshirt. For some reason, I felt like I viewed it from underwater. It got further away from me the longer I looked, too. And my palms stung. The phone stared up at me, lighting my face like a flashlight at spooky slumber-party story time.

"Bianca, you needed food and insulin almost an hour ago." Horace's hand covered mine, then nearly merged with it. I gasped.

He'd zinged me before with his energy, but we'd only mingled briefly before. This was the closest Horace and I had gotten to trying Possession. The last time I'd mentioned it, he'd shut the conversation down, so he had to sense an impending emergency to even go near that neighborhood.

My hand went into my bag, out of my control. I looked at Horace, watched his brows knit together and his jaw lock in concentration. What could he be working so hard at? Oh yeah, right. Moving my hand. That'd be difficult for a ghost to do all on his own.

"Ow!" I cried out at that old familiar pinch. The tiny insulin needle stung my right thigh, same side as the hand Horace had his literally in.

My hand moved again, back into my bag. I couldn't feel what my partner did with it but heard something rustle. Two voices flew past my ears with a gust of wind, then ghostly energy buffeted me back until I sat. My left wrist stung slightly as the pressure of my weight came off it.

"Unwrap it and eat." Horace's face looked more transparent than usual; all the effort must have drained him. He let go of my hand and the feeling woke in it again, all pins and needles like when my foot fell asleep.

I moved my left hand to cross over my right, feeling almost like it floated. Fingertips made contact with the shiny plastic wrapper. I let them catch and tear, then lifted whatever the snack was to my mouth and took a bite.

"Blargh," I said around a mouthful of PowerBar. "Not oatmeal. You know I can't stand the oatmeal-flavored ones."

"But it's got raisins in it." Horace's pale lips twisted into a half-smile as he finished the cheesy movie quote. "You like raisins."

"Not like this." I swallowed and took another bite anyway. "But it's okay. Thanks, Horace."

But my ghostly partner didn't smile. The medication and food had helped, I almost felt like I could get up. So why were his eyes like saucers? Why was Ignacius rushing toward us, looking like he was trying to spit fire? Didn't he know by now that dragon ghosts didn't get dragon powers? And why were Lynn and Blaine shouting from down the street?

I took one more chomp of the cardboard-textured PowerBar when one rough hand covered my mouth and the other snagged me around the waist. Whoever had nabbed me was strong enough to be a shifter—the scary and powerful kind. Possibly even of the big-cat variety. I stared down at my phone and the empty insulin syringe on the sidewalk, wishing I clutched either of them instead of the almost useless snack.

Wherever they were taking me, I could bet the food was worse than any PowerBar, even the oatmeal-without-raisins kind. Something soft and medicinal covered my mouth, and everything went dark.

Horace

I slapped a palm-full of my Psychic energy against the side of the car they'd dragged her into. I recognized the goon, too; this was the same Gatto gangster who'd answered the door for Tony's Trojan wiener ruse back in Olneyville. I pulled my arm back again, intending to deliver another blow to the sedan's chrome and steel hide but realized that'd be a waste of energy because I'd marked the car. I could track it later to wherever they took her.

I followed, feeling like a train in a tunnel, my handprint a rail and Bianca Brighton the light at the end of it. The car turned down a corner, out of sight, but that didn't matter. Only an Umbral Magus could hide it from me now. I don't know how many blocks I went before I felt a tug at my sleeve.

"Horace, we need a plan." Ignacius caught up, then passed me, floating backward in front of me when he realized I wouldn't stop.

"Find Bianca. Get her out of whatever trouble they've got in store for her." I stared through him. "Good enough for you?"

"No." Ignacius put his hands on his hips. "Wilfred's out finding a Redford, and in case you haven't noticed, the Gattos are solid. They're also shifters. How are we supposed to fight them?"

"We don't. It's a jailbreak."

"You can barely open a door in this state, let alone pick a lock." Ignacius shook his head. "Horace, what are we going to do if they put her in a root cellar? I can't burn a hole in the wall anymore, you know."

"So I'll go and get more help, and you'll stay with her while I do." I sped up, using my energy to push Ignacius aside. "Besides, I'm almost positive someone else can see us besides the mediums."

"You mean the diurnal owl and the pussycat?" Ignacius snorted. "That's like bringing a licorice whip to a gunfight."

"There's more to those two than you might imagine." I

glanced around. The streets had gotten grayer; they were filled with litter and had an aura of disrepair that countered the late-afternoon sun peeking through the clouds. "Olneyville again."

"It figures, right?" Ignacius pointed at the peak of a roof. "Haven't you been there before?"

"The Gatto Gang's newest real estate venture? Yeah, I've been here." I chuckled. "So, maybe Tony Gitano is the right guy to help us, but we need to do a couple of other things before calling in the cat and bird cavalry. Bet you can't keep up."

I surged ahead of Ignacius, leaving him behind for a few moments. I sensed him following me at a distance. Good. I'd need all the help I could get.

Bianca

I woke on a bare mattress in a room with ceilings so slanted, even someone of my stature risked hitting their head. When I looked around for a door, I found I couldn't focus on one corner of the room. The only apparent way in or out was a round window in one triangular corner, which had to be the inside of a peaked roof. The cooing of pigeons and the hiss of a distant radiator were the only sounds besides my own breathing.

Scrambling around, I checked every corner for the bag containing my insulin and the other three PowerBars I always carried. It wasn't there. I flopped back on the mattress, flinging one arm over my eyes. Then I cried.

I almost never did that. No matter how tired I got, or how much work I had to do on campus or with my courses, despair had become almost a foreign concept to me. Working with ghosts meant I knew there'd be something after death for me, something every medium understood. And I had plenty of friends amongst the ghosts and the solids. I also knew that things were better for incorporeals now than at any other time in recorded history. I wasn't afraid of death for its own sake.

But I was afraid of failing everyone else. Richard Hopewell was smart. He'd have a Psychic medium waiting in the wings to bind me into a contract and turn me against them. With someone like me on his side, an Extramagus could learn everything the Tinfoil Hatters had been up to these months. And they'd have no one to tell them to shut their traps around me, either. No one would be able to see me except Olivia.

"Don't cry, it's only a ghost." Horace was here. He only ever used that corny old joke when he found me weeping in the days after my accident when physical recovery was painful.

I moved my arm and sat up. My partner floated in front of the window, reminding me for all the world of a sheer curtain with the sun behind it.

"How did you find me?"

"Didn't. Marked the car and tracked you instead." Horace grinned. "Now that I know you're here, I'll be back. With help." I watched him sink below the lower curve of the window and hauled myself up, fingertips raking through the thick layer of dust on the windowsill as I peered after him.

A chill filled the air and I turned, putting my back against the wall.

"Youuuuuu…"

I stood my ground as something like a tattered old gray sheet rose through the floor. All the same, I had to choke down a lump in my throat the size of the hypnotoad before I could address my second visitor.

"Hi." I took a deep breath and spoke again to the wraith. "My name's Bianca Brighton."

"See…me?" It floated toward me until it hovered a bare inch from my face. I kept on reminding myself that it couldn't do anything to me, only to Magi or other ghosts.

"Yes." That was the understatement of the century. The holes in the wraith's incorporeal form yawned like chasms into oblivion. I looked at its left eye, the only persistent facial feature it had. "I'm a medium. Maybe I can help you."

"Not run?" Its voice came from what passed for its belly, under a scrap of what looked like faded blue gingham. "You run before."

"I'm staying this time." I folded my legs under me as I sat down on the mattress. "Anyway, I'm locked in. What about you? Why are you stuck here?"

The wraith's voice dragged out in an exhausted-sounding sing-song sigh. "Letter."

"That was why I came here the first time." Before I could squeak out the last word, the temperature in the room dropped until it felt positively arctic. "Our professor sent us to get it out of here and away from the Gattos."

"Waaaaatkins?"

"Yes."

The wraith sighed again, but unlike its earlier utterances, its voice droned on. It sounded like the ocean at high tide, breakers cresting but without the shoreline crash. The only way to explain what I heard and saw is that the wraith ran out like water down a drain. I'd seen full-fledged ghosts move on, and it looked nothing like what happened to the wraith. Moving on was a moment of contentment, sometimes even triumph. The poor wraith diminished into a puddle of what looked like tired relief.

I bowed my head for a moment, even though I knew I still wasn't alone. Another ghost approached; he was a familiar presence, although not as well-known to me as Horace.

"Am I late for something?" The ghost of Ignacius Harcourt floated through the wall behind me, then stopped and blinked as the remaining energy in the room dissipated. "Your fellow went for help, same as the windbag did earlier." Ignacius floated around, then stopped in front of me. "He's asked me to check on you before meeting back up with him later."

"My fellow?" I wondered what he meant. "As far as I know, I'm the poster child for the lonely hearts club."

"Ah, but you're not alone. You've got Horace Lancaster, of course." Ignacius held my gaze, then nodded. "I see. He never told you."

"Never told me what?" I blinked, then rubbed my eyes, getting sleepy again as usual.

"I can't say much more. That's for Horace to do." Ignacius sighed, his face lighting up with a smile. "Oh." That smile snuffed out like a candle. "What's wrong?"

"Um, Ignacius?" I sighed. "You've known me almost as long as Horace has. So, maybe you'll understand." I curled up on the mattress, pulling my knees up toward my chest to try to keep warm. "He tells me practically everything. We're best friends. So why won't he even let me discuss Possession? Is he worried about making things permanent? I mean, do you think he doesn't trust me?"

"You're partners. You ought to know better than I." Ignacius crossed his legs and sat, as if in a chair. I could just imagine the wingback chair he liked to sit in at the Nocturnal Lounge. "I'll only say it's clear that you two care a great deal for each other. Taking irrevocable steps in any relationship is hard. Perhaps he's waiting for the right moment."

"I wish he'd spill the beans already." I shut my eyes. "And you're the last person I'd expect to care about something like this."

"You call me a person instead of a ghost, and you still don't understand?" His voice sounded closer than it had been before.

"No. I'm Captain Clueless over here." I yawned, hoping my fatigue wasn't from lack of food or worse.

"We aren't just echoes, nuisances, or cheap labor as far as you're concerned, Bianca. You care about ghosts. It's only natural for ghosts to care about you." I heard a faint snort, then felt warmth blanket me, although no such thing existed in the corporeal version of the room. It would have been comforting if it hadn't also been ominous. Physically sensing something from a ghost who hadn't been a medium in life meant I might be closer to death than I'd originally thought.

"Why act like a sixth-grade go-between for Horace, then?" I opened my eyes. A translucent gray blanket, apparently made from ghostly smoke, covered me. I looked up at Ignacius. The corners of his eyes glimmered. Was he about to cry? "No, not like some school kid. Like a dad. But why?"

"Because I know what it's like to wait too long, and I can't help my own son with matters of the heart." Ignacius' features set into their usual expression of disdain, with a twist of wistfulness. "He can't see me, but you and Horace can, so I'm helping you instead."

I don't remember what I mumbled. Whatever I said sent a shimmer of translucent tears down Ignacius' face. I closed my own for a moment, then fought to open them again, worried that this might be the last time I'd see anything from my solid, living body.

Ignacius was gone. I was alone, just like Mrs. Donato had predicted. The blanket of smoke remained. I huddled beneath it, wondering what coincidence had in store for me next.

CHAPTER ELEVEN

Horace

I hurried. Ghosts, contrary to popular belief, couldn't just vanish themselves from one place to another all over town like Gnomes or Imps. We had to get from point A to point B like anyone else. Passing through walls wasn't always easy, either. The fact that I'd died at a relatively young age helped because I could vault over certain obstacles. No, not like Superman. More like some book character on a lonely island doing parkour.

Ghosts all along the streets stopped and stared. I let them, leaving them in the dust. I turned my back on the college as well. The only people who could help me were on the other side of the East Side, practically in Pawtucket. At my first glimpse of the clean, even lines of the Redfords' house, I felt relief wash over me. The place had a sense of security around it, one I usually associated with the Nocturnal Lounge. That's because it was a ghost-friendly place, of course.

I stopped at the bottom of the stoop next to Wilfred, who'd arrived before me. He seemed more transparent than usual. "Wow. Why do you look like a wraith bit a chunk out of you?"

"Had to outrun some trouble on the way over here." Wilfred shuddered.

"Trouble?" I put one hand in his shoulder and transferred a little of my own energy to perk him up a bit.

"Thanks." Wilfred sighed. "Some nosy old lady ghost started following me about a block away from the Senior Center. I had to walk through CVS, The Festival Ballet, and Seven Stars Bakery just to shake her. That audition for Swan Lake is no joke. Walking through the competitive vibes in there was like trying to navigate a hurricane in my old dragon form. And don't even get me started on hiding in the artisan bread oven."

"Oven-hiding sucks. Been there, done that, never again. But an old-lady ghost? Really?" I tried to remember whether any of the ghosts at the senior center had been old ladies. Of course, they had. It was the most popular hangout for extrahuman senior citizens. Duh.

"Yes." Wilfred scratched his head. "Something familiar about her, too. Couldn't put my finger on it, though."

"Familiar from where?" It was my turn to scratch my head. "You know what, never mind. We're here, and I know where Bianca is. Let's do this."

I hollered at the top of my ersatz lungs, knowing almost no one could hear me. I only sensed one medium in the house. A towheaded boy peeped through one of the windows on the second floor. I watched the smile fade from his face as the enthusiastically waving hand dropped. His brow furrowed, and I heard a click. He'd released the wards keeping most ghosts out.

Ed Redford stepped back as I floated up to the window and then through. I remembered how he'd been abducted, carried off to the Sidhe Queen's demesne back at the end of spring semester last year. Poor little guy had to be at least a bit paranoid after something like that. I dragged Wilfred along with me.

"Can you pop the ward up again please, Ed?" I nodded at the

window. "Wilfred said another ghost tried to follow him on the way over here."

"Okay." Ed shut his eyes, and a clack sounded as the wards snapped back into place. "What's up, Horace? You look like you've seen more ghosts than usual." The trace of a smirk pulled at one side of his mouth.

"Well, we've got trouble."

"Right here in Providence City?" Rob floated up through the floor, then pulled a funny face to make Ed bust out a full smile.

"Trouble that starts with an S, and it's a mess, and it stands for soul spindle." Wilfred managed all that with a straight face. My mouth dropped open as a sign of my deep respect for his song-parody skills.

"More than the usual kind?" Rob glanced past Wilfred and me. "Soul spindles barely exist nowadays. Are you sure it doesn't involve dragon arguments instead?"

"No. It's bigger and badder than stuff getting knocked over when ghosts get upset. Soul spindles are serious business."

"How so?" Rob turned his head, peering at me sideways. "They don't affect us ghosts unless we choose to tangle with them."

"Well." I paused for a moment, trying to remember what it was like to take a deep breath before rattling off a list of jargon I hoped Ed could understand. "The soul spindle is keeping an Astral Psychic out of his body, we've got Extramagus problems, the Gattos grabbed Bianca, and I think there's a medium helping the bad guys."

"Holy sh—" Ed slapped one hand over his mouth and immediately blushed. A muffled apology came from the other side of his fingers.

"If there was ever a time for you to cuss, kid, this is it. Because--" Rob opened his mouth, then closed it and shook his head. He shut his eyes and said, "It's okay."

Ed nodded, then took a deep breath. Rob wrung his

hands. Wilfred glanced around, then leaned in the doorway. Literally, at least by a fraction of an inch. He peered at Rob for a moment, then looked at me. I nodded. Wilfred and I had both spotted the same thing at the same time. Evidence of compulsion. Someone or something was definitely keeping the old haunt from talking, but Ed had missed the entire exchange.

"We have to rescue Bianca." Ed paced across the room between Wilfred and me. "Those Gattos went too far. I'm calling Tony."

"Don't." I shook my head. "At least, not yet. We don't have enough information to send the cat-man in, guns blazing."

"But aren't you afraid those goons will do something in the meantime?" Ed stopped with his hand an inch from the phone.

"Well, they took her for a reason. When I checked on her, they hadn't asked her to do anything yet." As I spoke, I noticed Rob heading through a portrait and then the wall behind it. It was odd, watching him slink away like that.

"Great." Wilfred snorted. "So, we've got no idea how much time we have."

"It's the middle of the afternoon, though." I pointed at the clock. "The Gattos are nocturnal, so we have a little time."

"Okay, then." Ed paced over to the middle of the room and closed his eyes. "Wait a minute. I already know about the Extra-magus. That's Richard. But did you seriously just mention a soul spindle?"

"Yeah." I stared at the kid, waiting for him to open his eyes. "One of those is the reason Nate Watkins can't get back in his body. We think the medium helping the Gattos is using it."

"Oh, no." Ed blinked, the lone tear trickling down his face reminding me of a sad cowboy. Which made sense, considering his dad had been one back in his early Under days, and this kid was his spitting image.

"Why am I suddenly getting a bad feeling about this?" Wilfred wrapped his arms around his chest, then shivered even though ghosts don't feel cold.

"Mama has had a soul spindle for about five months now. She's kept it down in the basement." Ed wiped that tear away, his pint-sized jaw setting itself into a defiant line. "I overheard her say she found it down at Water Place Park."

"Let me guess," I said. "It showed up right before the night the magipsychic amalgamation trashed the senior center's charity shindig."

"Yeah, well, and after that is when I noticed it had been activated." Ed blinked the last of the tears from his eyes, then swallowed. His nose was still red when he said, "So Mama's on the wrong side. She's helping Richard after all that?"

"Maybe, maybe not." I wasn't sure how to reassure a kid who might even know more than I did about this whole mess. "Possession can do crazy things to a Psychic medium if her ghost is stronger than her, you know."

Ed's eyes focused on a spot just above the top of the framed portrait. His voice sent a bolt of energy at the section of wall Rob had gone through earlier. "Rob. Get back in here."

"Woah, hold your horses, kid." The Colonial ghost wafted through the picture and hovered in front of it. The brown of his long coat obscured the face in the image. "I don't need to ask what this is about. You figured it out on your own."

"Damn straight." I put my hands on my hips. "How dare you take over and make the kid's mother help the guy who had him kidnapped?"

"I didn't." Rob took his hat off, revealing a shock of curly white hair. "I'm Ed's partner, not Delilah's. And it's permanent. The kid here can tell you more. He's not under a contract and matching compulsion to protect every member of this family." Rob peered at Ed. I'd given that look to Bianca on the mornings she tried to skip breakfast.

"Mama's old partner moved on back in March." Ed avoided

Rob's glare, blinking at Wilfred instead. "Something to do with you, Mr. Harcourt."

"What?" Wilfred's shoulders shook.

"Yeah, it was Caleb Jones. Remember him?"

"Name sounds familiar, but no." Wilfred shrugged. "I don't. Should I?"

"You rescued his son from a POW camp back in 1942. He wanted you to have a child of your own like you always wanted." Ed's lips turned upward, but the grin didn't touch his eyes. "Mama knew about you and Hertha's egg almost the same time as you did. As soon as Caleb found out, he moved on." Ed sighed. "After that, Mama teamed up with a little old lady ghost. They moved on to the Possession level before Mama wanted, but she needed to because Hertha called in a favor with her. Something about finding Edgar Watkins after she kicked Blaine out of the house."

"A little old lady ghost?" Wilfred straightened in the doorway. "That's who was following me on the way over here."

"Oh, no." I smacked my face so hard the palm went through it, remembering the name on Bianca's phone earlier. "No. Please tell me Delilah did not team up with Katherine Rogers. She was one of the most feared mediums back before the Reveal. She died this past spring, too. I saw the obituary on Bianca's phone."

"But why would a medium mess with an Astral Psychic like Nate Watkins?" Rob shook his head. "It makes no sense."

"It does if you understand it's the same reason Richard Hopewell stopped teaching at PPC and turned on the school." Another ghost floated up through the floor. His tusked mouth turned downward in a pout. I was more alarmed by his expression than the protruding teeth; everyone knew Samuel Kazynski had been one of the few trolls in the Sidhe Queen's court. "Your mother's partner is one of Richard Hopewell's aunts, and probably the most powerful Psychic medium in the history of the Rhode Island extrahuman community. Your mother either didn't remember who Katherine was connected to or thought she could overpower her."

"Holy…" Ed put his hand over his mouth, glancing at me before removing it to continue. "Hopewell."

"Nothing holy about the Hopewells besides their holier-than-thou attitude." Rob shook his head. "That's not their real family name, either. They changed it after Ignacius died fighting Richard's grandfather. That's not on the official Magus records, either."

"Are you serious?" Ed's voice shrilled with alarm. "How is there no record?"

"History, kid." I put one of my hands over his shoulder in what I hoped he considered a comforting gesture. "Not ancient, but distant enough for people to hide documents and wipe people's memories of them."

"So, is this why it's so important to find Edgar Watkins?"

"I assume so." Wilfred stared at the floor. "But my ideas don't matter. Drop the wards, please, Edward. I ought to make myself scarce."

"What's that supposed to mean?" Samuel crossed his arms over his chest.

"It means my wife started this particular mess by insisting Delilah take on a new partner too quickly." Wilfred sighed. "She just had to go poking the tip of her snout in, looking for information by proxy instead of doing it herself. The Gattos want Edgar too, you see. He wiped the memories of just about everyone who knew him. Only three of us got to keep our knowledge of his continued existence."

I wondered why Wilfred seemed to know about the old Memory Psychic when no one else did. Even Henry, Edgar's apprentice from before the Big Reveal, hadn't remembered him until he went looking for stored memories. Could that knowledge be the reason Wilfred got murdered?

Wilfred held out his hand as though he meant to ruffle Ed's

hair but stopped short. "Don't blame your mother. This mess is mine and Hertha's, and maybe Ignacius' too if old Mrs. Donato was right. She said we can't erase those problems, but we can still try to help your mother."

"But how?" Ed blinked up at Wilfred. "You're not ghostly mediums. Mama can kick yours and Ignacius' butts with one hand behind her back."

"They'll have help." I grinned at the kid. "As soon as Tony, Olivia, and I get Bianca out of Dodge, we've got this."

"Horace!" The shout came from outside the window. I turned to see Ignacius peering at us from the other side of the wards.

"I'll drop the wards for—"

"No time," Ignacius hollered. "Blaine and Lynn are both down-city at the PD."

"Well, that's good—"

"No, they're in custody." Ignacius shook his head. "Delilah Redford called in a tip, and now there's an APB out on half the kids we've been helping. I can't find Tony or Olivia anywhere. It's up to us ghosts to get Bianca out."

"I'm helping," said Ed.

"No way, kid." Rob waved a hand over his pint-sized partner's face. "It's naptime now. I'll give you the play-by-play later."

Ed shuffled over to his bed, practically asleep on his feet. He folded himself under a blanket, then let out a snore that sounded a bit like a purring tomcat. He pointed with one hand at the window. The wards dropped.

"I think I know where Tony and Olivia went." Rob gazed west out the window, toward Federal Hill. "I'll need help to see them, though. They might be under a glamour. Sam?"

"I'll help." The troll ghost floated toward Rob. Neither of them gave any explanation about why they thought a couple of shifters could cast a glamour, but I didn't care.

"We gotta go before he zonks all the way out." Rob jerked his chin at Ed. "If he's unconscious, the wards come back up."

The five of us sailed out the window, the tingle of the wards coming up behind us letting us know we wouldn't get back in until Ed dropped them again. We split off in different directions, Ignacius and Wilfred toward Rhode Island Hospital for the professor, Rob and Samuel toward campus to fetch the owl and the pussycat, and me back to Olneyville for my better half.

CHAPTER TWELVE

Bianca

Everything was fuzzy except the bare mattress beneath my calf. I wanted to reach down and adjust the left leg on my jeans so there'd be something between it and the scratchy polyester fabric and frayed ticking, but I couldn't. My limbs felt weighted down, as though I lay under one of the lead shields they put on you for x-rays.

Ignacius had gone, and so had his ghostly smoke. I figured he would, but being alone as everything started graying out at the edges had given me one last surge of fear. I knew it well—my old buddy survival instinct. But my body wasn't strong enough to respond with more than this vestige of consciousness. Soon, I'd be comatose. I wondered whether the Gattos intended that. Would whoever gave them their orders reward them or punish them for my probable brain damage or possible death?

I puffed out something like a dry laugh. This was the second time I'd approached this particular diabetic disaster. The first time, I'd become a medium. This time, I'd become a ghost.

"Should be three times," I croaked. "Charm."

Something thudded against the window. I couldn't turn my head to look before it hit twice more. The glass shattered and wood splintered, peppering my hair. I heard a scratch and catch of fabric, then watched a scaly, gray talon press the mattress in front of my face. It morphed, cracking like knuckles under pressure until it turned pale and delicate, its nails painted with moon-silvery gloss.

"Shh," Olivia breathed. She fumbled with stuff that rustled and then something tiny and shiny and filled with a clear liquid. I rolled my eyes to peer up at her. She'd just been an owl; couldn't have fit through that little round window otherwise. I figured I was hallucinating.

"I'm telling you guys, we have to move the ghost whisperer." Tony's voice came from somewhere through the floorboards. "There's a wraith here. What if she gets it to help her escape?"

"Nothing doing, kid," I remembered that voice from the Olneyville excursion. "And how would you know anything about haunts?"

Tony mumbled something, then I heard the smack of a fist on flesh. I wondered who'd been knocked out. Heavy footsteps pounded creaky stairs, stomping inexorably toward the door. Something clinked on the floor. The doorknob turned and Olivia dove on top of me like an extrahuman shield. I still couldn't move, not even when the door burst open and the goon with the yellow cat-eyes picked Olivia up by the neck with one meaty hand.

"Nothing personal, understand." The goon glanced down at me before smacking the owl shifter against one crumbled-plaster wall, then shook her like a terrier with a rat. "That goes for both of youse. You're known threats to my boss and his associates. If I don't take care of you, the whole place goes up in flames."

I had my answer to my earlier questions. I closed my eyes, ready for my own end, but not Olivia's or Tony's. They'd meant well, but I wished they hadn't come for me. They should have sent Blaine to roast this goon instead, but it was too late for regrets. Or so I thought.

"Bianca, you need to let me in."

"Horace?" The word went unspoken. I knew my lips hadn't moved. He wouldn't be able to hear.

"Yeah, in the ectoplasm." I felt his energy and imagined his hand on my shoulder.

I wished I could have opened my eyes to look at him, then banished the thought. But I'd see him soon enough once I crossed over. And if he could somehow hear my thoughts, I figured why not go ahead and communicate? "Can't. I'm on the way out."

"No. Stay put and let me in." I felt cold invade my limbs, shooting up them like cracks in melting ice. "Olivia dropped an insulin syringe. There's time to save everyone, but we have to share. I didn't want to because you'd find out I'm in love with you, and it's okay if, when I get there, I find out that you aren't. Saving your life is worth eternity in the friend zone."

Possession. I finally understood why Horace had waited so long. He had nothing to worry about, but I couldn't open my mouth to tell him so. I couldn't open my eyes, but I could still smile. I did and then moved my lips, thinking at him as hard as I could as though the words weren't enough, "Come in, then."

Bianca and Horace

Our eyes opened and we sat up, mingled Psychic energy surging through the living form that housed us both. We felt our cheeks heat as we understood the feelings we'd hidden until then. Later there'd be time to explore them, but our body needed insulin and other forms of safety first.

Our left arm swung down, fingertips brushing the dust off the floor along with what we needed to make ourselves well. One of us sighed and the other winced as the needle pierced the flesh on our belly, then we stood and swung the business end of the syringe at the goon's neck. We missed, exactly as planned.

He roared and spun, flinging Olivia at us. We ducked, catching a glimpse of bloodshot eyes and a gasping mouth before she crashed to the mattress. We knew she hadn't landed on the largest shard of glass because we had it in our other hand.

One of us hit the Mafioso with a sucker punch to the cheek and the other looked on in horror as blood pattered like rain to the cracked tiles between us. The droplets stopped, so we swung again, both of us ignoring the pain in our right hand. Even with the mitten on, we'd gotten a shallow cut.

The goon had hit the ground before our blow landed. We looked up into Tony's wide-eyed and somehow misshapen face. One of us realized his jaw was dislocated. We looked down to see a dagger coated in blood. He dropped it and rushed past us to Olivia.

"Copper?" Our voices came out mingled. Tony blinked at us and shook his head like his ears were ringing.

"Yeah." Even that one-syllable word came out garbled. Tony pressed one hand to Olivia's neck, feeling for a pulse. He clocked himself in the jaw with the other, then opened and closed his mouth. A hollow pop made us wince again. "Silver doesn't do it for cat shifters, but big or small, copper's a killer." He breathed out a relieved sigh, taking his fingers away from Olivia's neck but leaving behind a smear of blood. "Finally. You're both in there. 'Bout time."

"Yeah." One of us took up a defensive stance, getting between Tony and the bloodied copper blade. "You stabbed him." It wasn't a question from either of us.

"Had to." Tony closed his eyes. "It's the third time Paul tried to kill my friends. He won't die if EME gets here in time. Turn me in later if you want, as long as Olivia's safe."

We weren't sure what he meant by "later" because we intended to turn him in immediately. We reached for our phone before remembering it wasn't there. Tony knocked the glass from our hand and scooped up the dagger before we could stop him.

He didn't attack, just turned the knife's blade so he could wipe it on his shirt under that trench coat he always wore. The blood blended in with the black cotton fabric. We wondered how many times he'd hidden blood that way. Then, he sheathed it.

"Tony?" The rasp of Olivia's voice made us turn. "Oh, no. You didn't—"

"He'd have killed all three of us." Tony was by her side faster than he'd moved to retrieve his dagger. "But there's something more important we gotta do."

"Yeah, there is," we said. "Call the police."

"I said later." Tony grabbed Olivia's hand and turned. "Gotta get out of here before Dad's insurance policy hits the—"

An explosion downstairs cut him off. We scrambled to keep our feet under us as the floor tilted. The exterior wall cracked, shingled siding falling into the street, along with plaster and wood splinters.

"Out!" Tony grabbed our arm and pulled. "Move!"

"They can't fly!" Olivia's eyes went wider than usual. "Neither can you!"

"Don't matter." Tony hauled Olivia's arm, then let go, and she sailed out, fingertips stark against the twilit sky.

We fought. We grappled Tony's arm, trying to take him down with us if he insisted on defenestrating us. When the goon behind Tony groaned, we let him push. The last thing we saw before falling below the third floor was an angry Gatto holding Tony back from the edge. His thick arm stood out stark white against Tony's black coat and shirt. Tony's eyes bulged.

Our back hit something springy that bounced us back up. We sat, looking left to see Olivia holding out one hand to help us down from something we couldn't quite see. She looked just as confused about how it got there as we were. Our brow furrowed as we ran down the sidewalk after a glance back revealed the contraption's identity. Had it been under a glamour? But why? Who could have known ahead of time that people would fall out of that window? Before we could wonder how a trampoline had come to be on a side street in Olneyville, a wave of heat and light flared up behind us as the house burst into flames.

"Stand back!" Nox Phillips turned the corner, pulling a length of wood from her sleeve. It looked gray and weathered like dry and sun-bleached driftwood, but shone with a high-gloss as though it was wet. Flanking her were two Magi I recognized from school, bespectacled Ian and purple-haired Charles. Ian held a length of wood as yellow as a pencil in his right hand, and his left clasped Charles' right. Charles pointed a shimmering pink wand at the burning building and narrowed his eyes. "Move, already," he called in an almost sing-song voice.

We got out of the way, dragging Olivia with us. The frantic owl shifter flailed and screamed as she tried to go back toward the house after Tony. We couldn't let her. Tony's best chance was to let the Kelpie and the two Magi put the fire out.

Water rushing from Nox's wand increased the commotion. A gust of air from Ian's wand widened the spray, helping it spread out to reach more of the blaze. Charles kicked everything into high gear, amplifying Nox's stream to add even more water. Magically-enhanced water should have stopped any regular fire in its tracks, but there was nothing mundane about that conflagration. We pulled out the magipsychic monocle from our pocket and peered at the burning building. The fire was magical too, and even stronger than a Kelpie channeling water from the Deeps of the Under.

Nox cried out in frustration and stalked closer to the house than we would have dared. We watched Ian's knuckles whiten as he and Charles stepped up with her. A shadow blotted out the last of the daylight, and we looked up, expecting to see smoke. We blinked at the pair of jet-black dragon wings, then shivered as a rain of ice crystals blanketed the house.

The fire guttered and started to die. The house had mostly collapsed. Sirens sounded in the distance.

A howl rang through the air behind us as the alley filled with furred cavalry. A tall white wolf rushed past us, followed closely by a brown one who went on three legs. Flanking them were bears, one with deep brown fur and the other with a golden pelt.

One of us was baffled, the other understood that Josh Dennison, Tinfoil Hat's Alpha, had ordered the charge to rescue their fallen packmate. Josh's sister Beth pointed her nose at a pile of shingles and siding. The bear cousins, Bobby and Jeannie, got to work digging and shouldering past pieces of masonry the wolves couldn't have managed.

Josh howled, then red and blue lights painted the alley in an urgent display that reminded us of 3-D glasses—the old kind. We tried to hand Olivia off to Charles and Ian, but our body wouldn't cooperate. So we looked up, watching Ian's spectacles go from blue to red and then back again, his brow above the glasses a crinkling visual to match the aural crackle of a cellophane wrapper. What had he seen that we couldn't?

We ate the PowerBar even though it was the oatmeal kind with raisins. It took the edge off, giving a leaden lining to our ballooning head. Still, we weren't steady enough to stand, let alone help rescue Tony.

A stretcher rattled by, then another. An Emergency Medical Extrahuman barked orders sharper than claws. She waved a crystal pendulum over the spot at Josh's feet and a pale, still form levitated up from the wreckage.

We'll never forget the whisper-scrape sound Tony's tattered trench coat made as he floated toward the stretcher; it was like branches on windows. He turned his face toward us, gaze piercing ours until his eyes cut to Olivia. One side of his face was soot-streaked and pale beneath, the other blistered and cracked with burns. One corner of his mouth turned up as the stretcher rushed past, and his eyes closed. The second stretcher held a large, still form. Its face was covered.

One of us held Olivia tighter while the other's tears mingled with hers. The EME from the second ambulance bundled us inside, and the vehicle sped off after the first.

CHAPTER THIRTEEN

Bianca

In the back of the ambulance, Horace left my body. He poked his head into one compartment after another, finally pointing to one. I blinked at him, too fuzzy-headed still to understand what he meant, but Olivia got it. She pulled open the cabinet and handed me two cans of Ensure.

I popped the tops and drank them as the EME spied my medical alert bracelet and whipped out a glucometer to check my sugar levels. She peered at the tiny cut under my shredded mitten, then put a round band-aid on it.

"You're going straight to triage, kid." The Emergency Medical Extrahuman gave me the stink eye. I didn't blame her.

"Okay." I hadn't been taking proper care of myself for almost a month. If I had, maybe I could have escaped the Gattos on my own, and Tony would still be okay. I sighed, knowing I couldn't ask Horace anything about where he'd been in front of this strange EME, no matter how well-meaning she might have been.

"What's going on in the other ambulance?" Olivia put her

hands on her hips, swaying slightly as the ambulance took a corner.

"No idea." The EME didn't make eye contact with either of us. "You should sit. It's safer."

"Whatever." Olivia tossed her head, her nearly white hair cascading over her shoulder.

"That's information for his family to get first, anyway." The EME tossed her head right back at Olivia. It didn't have the same effect, what with her hair being piled on top of her head.

"That's what I'm afraid of." Olivia narrowed her eyes. "You know who he is, right?"

"That's not important." The EME put the glucometer away in a compartment. "We treat everyone who needs it."

"Oh, but it is." Olivia gave her a glare that could have withered a hundred-year-old oak tree. "Radio the PD."

"I'll follow procedure, thanks." The EME rolled her eyes again and turned her back to climb into the front of the van with the driver. "I've got it covered."

"Trust me, you don't." Olivia's lower lip trembled and her eyes got redder than they had been before, even with all of the earlier tears. I understood that she'd gotten fixated on Tony's situation. She wasn't thinking straight.

"Olivia, drop it." I tugged the strap of her satchel. "This isn't the battle you're looking for."

She sighed, then plopped herself on the padded bench next to me. I reached into her bag, pulled out her phone, and tapped it to wake it up. Olivia snatched the phone from me and began texting.

Horace peered over her shoulder. "Tell her to tell Lynn that Ismail needs to get to the hospital ASAP. I think Mrs. Donato's prediction about him matters now, and we know Jeannie's out of the Under."

"Thanks," Olivia said. "Got it." She typed faster.

"Wait." Horace blinked at her, then me. We'd both said the

same thing at the same time, even without the benefit of sharing a body.

"What?" Olivia didn't look up, just kept tapping.

"You heard Horace." I leaned forward to look at the perfectly human-looking eyes in her face. "Again. So it's not just some fluke from you coming off the meds."

"Yeah." She rolled her eyes.

"How?"

"I don't know." She lifted a shoulder, then lowered it. "I understand it's weird, though."

"Try unprecedented." Horace raised an eyebrow, tapping his foot on thin air.

"Does your shifter parent have odd abilities too?"

"No." Olivia had stopped tapping her phone screen, but she still didn't look up. "I mean, the people who raised me are just regular humans. They have no idea what kind of shifter I am besides what's obvious. I turn into an owl."

"But—"

"Look, this isn't the time or place to have a heart to heart. I'm adopted, okay?" Olivia put her phone back in her bag as the ambulance's engine cut out. "I've got a cat-man to worry about right now."

She opened the door, revealing the emergency entrance at Rhode Island Hospital. I followed her out, Horace floating along beside me. The EMEs from the ambulance called after us as they chased us into the ER. After that, they let us go. I could understand why. The triage nurse wasn't even at her desk because the place was a riot of living and ghostly chaos.

"Code Blue down from ICU!"

"Move him to Trauma Six!"

"Six is for transport, go Trauma Seven!"

Masked and gowned nurses and doctors dashed past, some with carts, others with gurneys. One of those held Tony, whose eyes stared at the ceiling, as blank as marbles. I turned my head, scanning all the ghosts. None of them looked like Tony Gitano. I could breathe again. At my side, Olivia let out a matching sigh.

Olivia pointed at another gurney. "Professor Watkins," she said.

I dragged her along as I went after the professor, but she took one long look over her shoulder as staff members wheeled Tony into Trauma Six.

Even though I couldn't get into Trauma Seven, the door had a window. I noticed that the silver thread at the professor's midsection looked thinner than it had the last time I'd seen him. His cheeks were pinched and ashen beneath the breathing mask they had on him.

"Come on!" Horace pointed at the line of silver trailing back down along the hall. We followed it, Olivia close behind us. I wasn't sure what she could do, but since she saw ghosts, maybe having her along was a good idea. It might be better for her, too. The alternative was standing around feeling useless while doctors tried to save Tony.

I followed the professor's silver thread out of the emergency department, down a flight of stairs, and past X-Ray and Imaging. Voices carried from the space under the door to a utility closet. I had recognized two of them before my hand grasped the doorknob.

"You have to stop this now." I opened the door to see Ignacius holding his hands out in front of him, palms facing Mrs. Redford. "Nathaniel Watkins will die if you don't let him go back to his body. You're not a killer, Mrs. Redford."

"Delilah's not in…charge, you know." The woman chuckled. "She hasn't been for most of the time, in case you haven't noticed."

It all made sense now. Delilah Redford's ghostly partner had taken over her body almost completely. That was the reason she'd sounded like a different person giving her lectures, but not like two people talking at the same time as Horace and I had.

This ghostly medium, whoever she was, had gotten the upper hand. Delilah had probably been losing time and experiencing blackouts. Everything made sense now.

Of course a ghostly medium trapping her host wouldn't be able to compel other ghosts, so that's why she called me into her classroom to do it. And it explained Rob's weird behavior. He must have been trying to rat her out, but couldn't due to his familial contract with the Redfords. Or Delilah had flat-out banned the Colonial ghost from talking about her partners at some point.

"Okay, then." Ignacius took one step toward her. "Just let Wilfred and Nate go. Take me instead. We left some big issues unsettled between us, right, Katie?"

I blinked, then looked up. Delilah Redford's right hand was in her pocket, but the left was raised above her head, clutching a shiny blue crystalline object—the soul spindle. How had I not noticed she'd been using the wrong hand all month? Mrs. Redford wasn't a southpaw, but apparently, this Katie person was. I blinked again, wondering how in the world Ignacius knew her.

"You, of all people, should know how I feel. We ought to be ruling this world, not slaving away in it." Five silver threads protruded from the object in Katherine's borrowed hand; one was the professor's, which I'd followed in from the hall. The other four held Wilfred and Nate to the ceiling. The strange blue aura surrounded them both. I'd never seen anyone use a soul spindle. I shivered.

"You lived through the Reveal, Katie." Ignacius reached toward her with one hand. "You know that's not right anymore. This world belongs to the humans as much as it does to the extrahumans. Helping some crazy Extramagus isn't going to change things back."

"I don't want things back." Katherine shook Delilah's head. "I want to see progress in the right direction, the one where the most powerful rule. People like Richard Hopewell. People like the man you were before you had to marry the poisonous egg factory. People like your son, if he'd only grow the stomach for it."

"That's got nothing to do with Wilfred or Nate, Katherine." Ignacius took a step forward.

"It does, though." She sighed. "They meddled too far, both of them. Wilfred with his heroics during wars he should have focused more on profiting from, and Nathaniel by softening this new generation toward the mundanes. The Rogers family Psychics swore an oath to help the Hopewells. You know that. Letting these two go makes his Quest harder."

"Katie, please. If you ever loved me, let them go. Delilah, too. You know she's got a kid at home, and he's worried sick about her. I promise to stay with you this time. Nothing's stopping me, not now when we're both like this."

"I'm afraid I can't do that, Iggy. Letting them go, I mean. But you're right. I'll take you up on that offer to stay with me for old time's sake." Delilah's mouth curled in a sneer unlike any of her usual expressions. A sixth silver thread emerged from the top of the bright object in her hand. As it shot toward Ignacius, a seventh protruded from the bottom.

"Do something!" Olivia's voice came from behind me in the hall.

I stepped into the room, even though I had no idea what I could do while saddled with a body. If only I could have gone out like Nate, I might be able to fix this mess, but I was a medium, and we couldn't project. As a solid, I couldn't touch the silver threads.

I thought about something Professor Watkins had said in Incorporeal Studies class. Technically, I was wrong about projecting. Any medium could choose to leave their body, but nothing would keep it alive. If I did that, I'd die in moments, but would that be long enough for me to stop Kate? Then my partner rushed in once again, intending to save me and all the other incorporeals in the room.

"We'll do this together." Horace winked at me, took my hand, and stepped into my body. This time, I stepped out.

Horace

I couldn't feel Bianca this time. The shock of being in her body without her presence mingling with mine almost jolted me back out, but I held on when I saw her beside me, as translucent as I had been on the day I'd died. I felt the connection between us like I had when we'd shared her body before, but stronger. I knew I was her anchor and had to hold the door open for her to get back in. If I left or got expelled, we'd both be ghosts.

I hadn't expected her to go that far, but it made sense. Only a ghostly medium could touch ghosts who hadn't been mediums in life, but only a living Psychic medium could use a contract anchoring a ghost to sever other ties. Technically, at that moment, Bianca was both.

"Wilfred! Ignacius! I call you to duty!" Bianca snapped her fingers, the tip of one not even pushing through the other as their contact made a percussive sound. I checked for a silver thread, but there was none. She wasn't drawing strength from her body like Professor Watkins had. She was a real ghost and just as strong as Rob, who'd been one for hundreds of years. I blinked, then remembered to close Bianca's mouth. It was slow going. I'd nearly forgotten how to move a solid body without Bianca's recent experience to draw on.

The silver threads binding the dragon ghosts frayed and fell apart. Delilah bellowed in a voice not entirely her own, calling on more energy to power the device again. She opened her hand to reveal more of the soul spindle. Faceted like a cut-glass door-knob, it glowed light blue. It reminded me of moths dive-bombing a bonfire. I found it both entrancingly beautiful and utterly terrifying.

Bianca flexed her hands and steel-looking gauntlets covered them. I'd taught her well about how ghost's bodies responded to their willpower. She reached up, grasping at the threads that held Nate Watkins to the ceiling. Wilfred moved to help, and I noticed he looked tattered, worn, and frayed around the edges. Being bound up in the soul spindle had cost him. If he went back at it again, he could lose too much of himself and become a wraith.

Ignacius noticed, too and brushed past Wilfred. "Stick around and watch your egg hatch, windbag," he said. His hands sprouted thick red scales and his nails lengthened into claws. It had to be enough to protect him, I thought.

Together, Bianca and Ignacius pulled the threads. They screeched against Bianca's gauntlets like razor wire on steel. Ignacius' claws tore the thread, but it cut into his scaled hands. He bared his teeth and soldiered on, willing energy from his lower half into his lacerated hands. The threads stretched as thin as spider silk, approaching a breaking point.

"Now, Olivia!" Bianca's voice rang out as the first of the threads around the professor snapped.

The owl shifter screeched, making the hairs on the back of my borrowed neck stand on end. Olivia tackled Delilah Redford, knocking her into a boxy steel cart. I saw her eyes go amber and wider than a human's could. She screeched again and batted Delilah's blue left hand, and I understood what she was trying to do—break the Psychic's contact with the spindle.

"This is for Watkins!" Olivia managed to knock Delilah's wrist against the cart. The spindle clinked on the floor, but Olivia was too enraged to bother with the spindle. "And this is for Tony!"

That night, I decided I'd cross any other kind of shifter before I'd piss off an owl. Spacy, petite, bookish Olivia Adler now resembled legendary descriptions of Harpies. She screeched again and drew back her foot to swing it at Delilah's head, except she didn't just kick Delilah. Somehow, she also managed to kick the ghost possessing her.

The ghost of Katherine Rogers landed directly on the soul spindle, and her mouth and eyes stretched like an empty electric socket. She flickered with Psychic and ghostly energy, reminding me of old reel-to-reel projectors when the lightbulb inside was starting to go.

I almost took a step back. Instead, I glanced up. Nate floated, propped between Bianca and Ignacius, free of the threads. The only one connected to him now came from out in the hall and led back toward his body. I stepped forward instead, bent my borrowed knee, and punted the soul spindle. It landed next to Delilah's prone form.

"Transport to Trauma Seven," said the intercom. They'd stabilized the professor's body, then.

I breathed a sigh of relief too soon. Katherine Rogers had become a wraith, and she was heading for the strongest ghost in the room—Bianca.

I stepped forward, but Ignacius moved faster. He'd always moved fast for a ghost. Maybe it had something to do with being able to fly while he lived.

I thought we'd end up having to deal with two wraiths, but light poured from the wounds Katherine's wraith dug in Ignacius, and finally, I understood. Ignacius hadn't been waiting for Blaine to grow up or for Hertha to die. Like many dragons, he hadn't been permitted to marry his destined love because a Precognitive Psychic had predicted he'd make full-blooded dragon babies with someone else. A woman named Katherine Rogers had been his unfinished business. Ignacius was moving on.

He embraced his Katie like a groom taking the bride in his arms. The ghost of Ignacius Harcourt smiled down at Wilfred and mouthed something that looked like "Thanks, windbag." The light pouring out of him banished all the shadows in that dingy old utility closet as he moved on. When everything dimmed back down to normal, I saw that Katherine's wraith had moved on with him.

Bianca left Nate with Wilfred and covered her eyes with her hands. I knew it didn't stop any incorporeal from seeing, but that wasn't the point. I put my arms around her, hugging my partner back into her body with me and answered her grief with love, all I had to give her. It never ran out because she kept giving it back.

We spun on our heel as the door slammed. Olivia had left the closet. We heard her voice both in our ears and over the intercom in the hall, declaring a Code Silver to the utility closet in X-Ray and Imaging. We separated and hurried out the door, leaving it open behind us so responders would find Delilah, and took off after Olivia.

CHAPTER FOURTEEN

Bianca

"Olivia, wait up!" I hurried after her, surprised to see such a short girl moving so fast. The owl shifter was full of surprises that night.

When I caught up, she didn't even look at me. I understood why when the intercom chimed again, followed by a page for Mr. Gitano. We pushed through those service doors back into the ER, hugging the walls to stay out of the way and hopefully beyond notice. Horace surged ahead with Wilfred and the professor. They sailed into Trauma Seven, where, through the window, I saw them help Nate Watkins back into his body. A nurse and a doctor gave each other a high five at his bedside. I saw a flash of fangs in the doctor's mouth.

The scene in Trauma Six was something completely different. The doctor stood there with her mouth open. The nurse's eyes narrowed into two angry lines, and his jaw clenched. A man stood at the window, his eyes yellow and self-satisfied in a way that reminded me of the stepmother's cat from Disney's Cinderella. He pressed a clipboard against the glass.

"Call it." The words tumbled from this doctor's mouth like plaster from the wall of that triple-decker in Olneyville. The rosiness of exertion vanished from the doctor's face, leaving behind only a dull and sickly bronze color.

"Time of death, twenty-thirteen." The doctor shook her head, pulling one glove after the other off and tossing them into the trash.

Beside me, Olivia Adler stopped breathing. Her hand clutched at the thin air between us, so I put my hand there. She snared it in a grip like a magic lasso. "No," she finally breathed. Then the man at the window turned around.

I saw the paper on the clipboard first; the header read DNR Order. It was signed and notarized, all the Is dotted and all the Ts crossed. The date was last March, after Gattos took potshots at Blaine and Kimiko over Spring Break. It had Tony's name on it.

After that, I noticed Mr. Gitano's shoes and clothes. Expensive Italian leather, practically brand new. Armani pinstripe, black and blue. Powder-blue shirt, and blood-red tie with a pin in the shape of a spear.

His entire body was thick with muscle; even his jaw looked like it could crack artillery shells. The man in the suit glanced at me and then Olivia, his gaze lingering on her face. His coloring matched Tony's, but the resemblance ended there. Our friend's slight stature, wiry muscles, and fine-boned facial features must have come from his mother's side of the family.

Horace got between Olivia and Tony's father. "Don't."

"I wasn't expecting to meet you here, Mr. Gitano." Olivia's eyes went amber and round again. I squeezed her hand.

"Oh, but I was expecting to meet you." Mr. Gitano's voice wasn't gruff or gravelly, as I had expected. Instead, it was a warm tenor, as smooth as butterscotch. "I hope to see you again soon at the wake, the Mass, and the graveside. You meant a great deal to my son, Miss Adler, though perhaps you weren't aware."

"I wasn't until just a short while ago." Olivia's grin made me shiver with fear for her and of what she might do. "I'll be there. For him. Count on it, Mr. Gitano."

Tony's father turned his back, saying nothing more. He pushed through the swinging double doors into the lobby. A black Cadillac sedan sat idling outside the automatic glass doors beyond. The goon who'd been there that first night in the Olneyville house, the one Tony had called Paul, occupied the front passenger seat.

In the back was a young woman, her head covered with a pashmina shawl. She turned her head, then hung it when she saw me. I almost didn't recognize her because her face looked fuller, although her eyes had sunk as though she'd gained weight and become exhausted. It was Cassandra Spanos. The Gatto Gang's uncanny timing made total sense now.

Olivia and I turned in tandem, looking back through the window of Trauma Six. Tony's body was covered with a sheet and an orderly fiddled with the brakes on the gurney. A nurse sat at the island of a desk in the middle of the ER, typing with one hand and kicking back coffee with the other. His eyes were red with unshed tears. I looked all around for Tony's ghost, but I couldn't find him anywhere. Horace met my eyes and shook his head; he hadn't seen Tony either.

"Tony's ghost isn't here." Olivia gazed at me without blinking. "Now, why is that?"

"Where is he?" I turned. Ismail had pushed through the doors from the lobby, Jeannie La Montagne following close behind.

"Sir, you can't be in here." The nurse stood up and jogged around the desk. "Please wait in the lobby." He looked down his nose at Olivia and me. "Same goes for the two of you."

"I'm Duke Ismail of the Goblin King's court, my great-grand-son's in here, and I'm contesting the DNR filed by his—" The djinn stopped as he caught a glimpse of what was going on in Trauma Six. "No."

"Sir, I'm sorry, but his father just left a minute ago." The nurse sighed. "I'm not sure life support would have helped anyway." The nurse went on to direct the bunch of us to the hospital chapel.

On the way, a ghost waved me over. She was the same lady Yoshi Ichiro had sat on just a month earlier in this same hospital. "Go and see your Psychic Professor friend." She jerked one thumb at a hallway. "He's in there, room 1409."

I left Ismail with Jeannie, glancing back over my shoulder as they pushed through the chapel doors. Olivia followed me, her eyes shining with anger glossed over with unshed tears.

Across the hall from 1409, we watched through the window as a nurse pressed buttons on a beeping monitor. Nate Watkins rolled his eyes, waving one hand to get her attention. He pointed at us and said something. The nurse shook her head, and he gave her his most withering professorial stare. She took a half-step back, nearly tripping over her own feet. After that, she paced across the hall toward us.

"Go in and see him, then." The nurse crossed her arms over her chest. "You have five minutes."

"Thanks" I smiled, and the nurse's jaw loosened a bit. As Olivia and I went, I heard her mumble something about visiting hours and rest.

"Professor, I'm so glad you're—" I shut my mouth when he opened his.

"Did you get that document out of the house before it went up?" Professor Watkins pointed at my plaster-dusted clothes. His voice croaked like a toad, and he fumbled for a cup of ice chips at his bedside. I picked it up and held it to his lips. The professor closed his eyes for a moment.

"Yeah." Olivia put her hands on her hips. "The night you told us about it, they went and got it. We've been trying to translate it ever since."

"Oh, for crying out loud!" The professor's arms twitched. I guessed this was the post-coma equivalent of him throwing his hands up in frustration. "You opened it, got your tiny minds stumped, and went all that time without coming back to ask me questions?"

"Pretty much." I tapped my foot on the floor. "You didn't tell us to come back."

"I didn't what?" He blinked. "Oh, crap. I'm as off the ball as half the new crop of freshmen." Nate Watkins hung his head. "That means that all this and Tony—it's all my fault."

"No." Horace hovered at my elbow. "It's not. Projecting Psychics lose track of things when they're out of their bodies for too long."

"Look, Professor—" I hesitated, not sure whether Horace's information would bring comfort or more shame. Professor Watkins might think he was at fault somehow for getting tangled up with a soul spindle in the first place.

"It's Richard Hopewell's fault." Olivia took the ice cup from me. She gently held it out to him and the professor lifted his face, revealing tear-smeared cheeks. "After that, you can blame his own father. Blame the ghost of Katherine Rogers for selling us all out and manipulating Mrs. Redford. Blame Ignacius' ghost for not warning us about her. And then, if you want to get picky, blame Tony for playing the hero, and blame me for not grabbing him when he pushed me out of the building. Blame the wise guy who attacked him. But don't you *dare* blame yourself."

"Fine. I'll stop the blame game." The professor's words didn't carry their usual snark; he just sounded exhausted. He looked at the ice cup and shook his head.

"That's good." I nodded at him, then Olivia. She backed off. "Look, we never figured out exactly what was on that paper. Are you going to tell us what it is?"

"It's a contract." Nate Watkins stared at nothing. "You're not supposed to be able to translate or decrypt it. It's in Goblinese."

"But we found your name on it." Olivia tapped her chin. "Your brother's, too. Those were the only words Kimiko could decrypt."

"Of course, she did because there's no Goblinese equivalent for our names." Professor Watkins sighed. "It's a contract between the Goblin King and us. Edgar's old lady, too. We agreed to kick ass and wipe minds back in the day."

"Why?" Olivia tapped her chin with her index finger.

"It's all pointless now, so I guess I can tell you." He closed his eyes. "It was all because of some shifters. Magical ones, both born in the Under."

"Like Kimiko and Blaine?" Olivia blinked.

"Nothing so common as a Tanuki or a dragon." The corners of the professor's mouth turned up. "Although Edgar wiped some events connected to a couple of those on Hertha's orders. I can't say a word about the other one, but Tony wasn't just a regular cat shifter. He was something different. Maybe new. Or maybe old and back again after ages and ages. I'm unclear on that part from the out-of-body brain fog. It doesn't matter now that he's dead, though."

Horace tugged my sleeve, and I looked up to see the nurse heading back across the hall. I had to make sure of something, but Olivia got a question out before I could.

"You're going to testify? Exonerate Brodsky?" Her hands were curled into fists, knuckles whiter than her hair.

"Yeah, Adler." Professor Watkins leaned his head back against the pillow. "You kids kept your word. So will I."

"Good." She stalked out of the room, opening her hands to fish out her phone again. I noticed bloody crescents in her palms, left by her nails.

"Get some rest, Professor. And thanks for seeing us." I followed, Horace floating along beside me.

"Thanks for saving me." Nate Watkins' voice was barely a whisper.

The nurse brushed past me, and I understood. The medical staff had no clue that their patient coding had to do with a vengeful ghost, and the professor wanted to keep it that way.

Whatever secrets he and his brother had been required to keep, some still had to go unspoken. Their full plans and preparations had yet to unfold.

I heard Olivia on the phone, asking Mr. Ichiro about a witness protection police detail for Professor Watkins. When we'd been here last month, I wouldn't have thought it necessary. Now, I knew it was essential. Clearing Brodsky meant law enforcement would look harder for Hopewell, not that they wouldn't want to hear about who blew up Mr. Gitano's house in Olneyville. All that magical fire would trace back to the Extramagus, adding up with the attempt on Lane Meyer's life over the summer.

Olivia waited for the police while I went back to the chapel. On my way, I saw two familiar faces, Detectives Weaver and Klein from the Newport PD. Klein smiled, showing off his fangs as he gave me a cheery wave. Weaver nodded at me instead, her hands occupied with slapping handcuffs on Delilah Redford. An ECSI held an evidence bag with the soul spindle inside. I figured there'd be someone for me to testify about and exonerate months down the road, just like Professor Watkins.

At the chapel, Ismail and Jeannie had finished speaking with the chaplain. I explained everything as best as I could on our way back to campus. I hadn't known for sure that Ismail and Tony had been related, and I made myself a promise that night to follow my hunches more closely. Things might have gone differently if I had acted during tea with Mrs. Donato.

Olivia's ban against the blame game would have been easier to bear than the truth, but it wasn't something I could get behind completely. We all shared responsibility for losing our friend. Owning it meant being better next time, which was important because the rest of us were still in danger.

The Nocturnal Lounge was packed with Tinfoil Hatters, all waiting for news about Tony. When they got it, they dissipated like helium from a sinking balloon. I looked around for Olivia, but she still hadn't arrived.

"Horace, we need to find her. She shouldn't be alone right now." I didn't have to explain who and what I meant. He just understood as he always did.

"Okay, let's go." Horace pointed at my phone. "Text her just in case, though." I did.

I traversed campus, asking everyone I encountered. No one had seen Olivia. She hadn't messaged me back, either. I shuffled over to a bench near the dining hall and turned around to sit.

"Watch it, big'un!" The voice came from the seat.

"Um, sorry?" I turned back around to find an empty bench.

"Down here!"

"Oh!" A tiny figure in a tall, pointy, brimless hat with a bushy beard peered up at me with beady eyes. "I'm sorry. I haven't seen a Gnome in a long time."

"Because you don't look in the right places!" They cleared their throat. "The most clueless Psychic on campus is Bianca Brighton, but I think that's changing. Your friend's at the hospital still. Look there."

"Thank you," I said just before the Gnome vanished with a pop of displaced air.

I headed back to Thayer Street, hoping it wasn't too late to catch a bus back to Rhode Island Hospital. As I stood waiting, a white Volvo pulled up. The passenger-side window rolled down to reveal Sir Al in the driver's seat.

"Get in, please." The Sidhe knight's polite words didn't match the urgency in his voice.

"Rhode Island Hospital?"

"Yes!"

I got in on the passenger side, Horace hovering in the back.

CHAPTER FIFTEEN

Horace

"What do you mean, you can't complete the autopsy?" Captain Linda Dennison narrowed her eyes at the Medical Examiner.

"I mean exactly what I just said." The gangly man in the white coat folded his arms over his chest. "I can't finish the autopsy on Tony Gitano."

"But you have to." Olivia Adler waved a piece of paper. "The law requires it in cases like this, where foul play is suspected."

Bianca squeezed past Olivia through the doorway, walking softly until she got to the row of tables beyond where the Providence PD captain locked gazes with the ME, whose mouth opened and closed like a fish out of water. All of the stainless-steel tables stood empty. Bianca looked at me and I nodded, then raced through the air and stuck my head in each freezer.

I found mostly empty slabs, but a few people. None of them were Tony Gitano.

"He can't autopsy a body that's not here anymore." I floated behind the ME and blew a raspberry at him. Rob would have been proud.

"Why aren't you telling the captain that Tony's not here?" Bianca paced over toward one slab, beside a tray with slightly bloody surgical tools arrayed across a green cloth.

"Is this true, Gary?" Captain Dennison put her hands on her hips, her eyes going yellow and wolfish a moment later. "You lost the body in a murder investigation allegedly linked to the Gatto Gang?"

"I don't know what happened." The medical examiner's face paled until he resembled a vampire. He wasn't one. "I went to stow a piece of copper that broke off the murder weapon, and when I came back—" He jerked his chin at the empty table, then shivered. "There's no such thing as zombies, so I don't know what happened."

"Well, have hospital security send me the surveillance video tonight." She waved one hand at a camera on the wall. And give me that evidence you extracted." The captain dropped her hands to her sides, then leaned forward. "Now!"

Gary the ME jumped. I would have too if I'd been on the receiving end of a werewolf's anger. He sprinted across the room, grabbed a plastic evidence bag, and handed it to Captain Dennison immediately. She held it up to the light, peering at the object inside. I joined her.

The bag contained more than half of a copper blade. I recognized it right away, of course. So did Bianca and Olivia, judging from their gasps. It was the business end of the dagger Tony had used to attack the goon back in the Olneyville house. Somehow, the wise guy had turned Tony's own blade on him.

"Fax over all the written observations you have." The captain's nostrils flared as she took a deep breath. "And you find that body. Without it, we have no case against his dad. Habeas corpus, Gary. You know the drill."

Captain Dennison stalked out of the room, holding the bag. Gary's shoulders dropped as he let out a sigh of completely understandable relief. Then he hung his head.

"Is he still alive?" Olivia's question came out in a voice more strained and frayed than the broken end of the dagger. "Could he have gotten up and left on his own?"

"There's no way." Gary shook his head. "He'd been dead for hours. Once the heart and brainwaves stop, shifters can't do their fast-healing thing."

"But maybe the dagger was keeping him in a near-death state or something." Olivia Adler grasped at a tattered remnant of hope.

"Look, if the doctor upstairs had thought to look for copper, they might have saved him. It's one reason we need more MDs who specialize in extrahumans. But the education hasn't caught up with the law yet." Gary hung his head. "With that blade in his chest, he couldn't heal the burns or his liver or the punctured lung."

"I don't believe you. The simplest explanation for Tony disappearing is that he got up and walked out." Olivia spun on her heel. "Come on, Bianca, Horace. We've got a cat shifter to track."

The owl shifter strode out the door ahead of us. I didn't agree with Olivia's explanation. We followed at a decent distance, not far enough away to lose her but not close enough that she'd overhear.

"Denial isn't just a river in Egypt," I whispered to Bianca. "It's a stage of grief."

"I know." Bianca ran a hand through her hair. "But I don't think she'll ever believe Tony is really gone unless we find his body."

"Do you think the simplest explanation is that one of the Gattos took him?" I peered at her, taking in the smooth lines of her face in profile as she contemplated my theory.

"No, actually." Bianca frowned. "His ghost isn't anywhere to be found, so I think it's much more likely that someone took his body to the Under. The Gattos can't do that."

"But Hopewell's a changeling. He could have taken Tony

there." It all started making sense. "He knows what we can do, and he doesn't want to give us any more ghostly allies. If Tony's ghost got trapped in the body by the copper blade, then taking his body away immediately after it got removed would mean he's stuck down there."

"Yeah." Bianca nodded. "Even if someone like Fred or Sir Al found his body down there and brought it back, Tony's ghost would still be stuck without a monarch's permission to leave. And with Ignacius having moved on, there's one less pair of eyes on our side."

We walked out through the sliding glass doors at the front of the hospital. I kept pace with Bianca, focusing my energy on my hand so she'd feel it against hers. She turned her head and gave me a shaky smile and moved her fingers so they curled around where mine would have been. As insubstantial as I was in her world, she made an effort to help me feel I belonged in it. I understood hope and how it intersected with love because Bianca had helped me learn how, and while I couldn't agree, I didn't blame Olivia Adler one bit for her irrational reaction to Tony's death.

"Olivia's tenacious." I focused my energy on our mingling hands. Bianca sent a current of her own back. The resulting tingle reminded me of how much closer we were now. How much more connected, and what that meant. "And she's a woman in love. I happen to know that's a powerful combination." I gazed at her. "What do you expect her to do? Give up?"

"I expect her to figure out what actually happened, no matter how painful the truth might be." Bianca sighed. "She's got a ton of work ahead of her. Helping Mr. Ichiro will probably be the easiest part."

"Do you think the truth will hurt her so much?" I raised an eyebrow.

"Olivia specifically?" Bianca looked up at the sky where the moon hung like a lopsided alabaster bowl. "Most of the time, truth is like that—nothing but pain, especially if you have to face it alone. And right now, she thinks she does."

"Good thing we've got each other." I sent a second surge of energy to my translucent hand, knowing she'd feel a cool tingle.

"Yeah, we're the lucky ones." She did the same, sending back a warmth I'd almost given up on experiencing.

"Do you think Olivia can handle her classes, the trial, and investigating what happened to Tony?" I had my own ideas, but I wanted to hear hers.

"I don't know. She might not be going against Hopewell and the Gattos with Tony like she'd want, but she won't be alone." Bianca picked up her pace and caught up with her friend. "She's got the law on her side, and all of us, too. I guess we'll have to wait and see exactly what she does."

We didn't have to wait long.

WANDS OUT

A PROVIDENCE PARANORMAL COLLEGE
SHORT STORY

Charles and I followed Nox Phillips, running as fast as we could to get there in time. I knew she needed our help to rescue Bianca Brighton and Olivia Adler, but she'd never said from what. Charles didn't care, but I'm his better half for a reason. I question everything.

At the corner of the block, we saw a blast of light. Even from this far down, I felt its heat and force. I pushed against it with my Air magic instinctively, which let us keep running. Before we turned down the alley next to the shattered building, Nox drew her wand.

"Good thing we slept in today, Ian." Charles dropped me a wink.

"Yeah." I grinned at my boyfriend. "We got more sleep than most EMEs."

The smoldering building caught fire, going up quickly. Olneyville had loads of old buildings, and this one was no exception.

"No, Ian!" Nox's command stopped my initial reaction to cut and run.

Charles gripped my free hand and his warm comfort eased my fear.

Figures fell from the window and hit something springy. Their contact with the item revealed it—a trampoline. Professor Thurston had explained this just the week before. A glamour, one I knew Nox hadn't cast. She grasped her wand.

"Stand back!"

Charles and I drew ours, ready to help. Good thing, since she used hers to blast the burning building. We'd been doing exactly this type of exercise in the Advanced Magical Theory Lab on a smaller scale. I added my air to her water, turning the effect into a pressurized blast. Charles used his to dial the water and pressure up to eleven.

"Move, already!" I knew my boyfriend rolled his eyes even though his face turned toward the building instead of me. His tone gave him away.

The people who'd fallen scurried away, making way for the person Charles had seen up there, who was still waiting to evacuate. A humanoid figure appeared at the hole in the wall. I recognized him right away by his trench coat and scuffed Converse All-Stars. Tony Gitano. I ignored the screams coming from my left as I watched the reason for them. A shadow fell on Tony from inside the building.

Nox screamed, an incoherent cry of defiance against the fire. She moved up closer to the building, and our combined magics took Charles and me with her. The water we put out increased exponentially. I felt the surge of Faerie magic. The fire should have taken a hit then. Instead, it increased.

The shadow behind Tony solidified into a shambling brute of a man. Built like a linebacker but moving like a Romero zombie, he was the stuff of nightmare. His tattered suit smoldered, skin scorched from the bone on one side of his face. His right hand held a blade that gleamed orange, either copper or lit by the fire, I couldn't tell. What I could see was that he'd pulled the knife out of Tony's pocket and that it had a pointed tip and sharp edge.

Olivia was flailing in Bianca's grasp. Her hair covered her face, wild and desperate, and I understood. She loved Tony, and would do anything to get him out of that building alive. If it were Charles up there with me scared senseless, I'd want Olivia to warn him for me.

I opened my mouth to shout a warning to Tony but didn't have the strength to get more than a whisper past my lips. I felt like an utter failure, so I gripped my boyfriend's hand tighter, and my wand too. If I couldn't warn Tony Gitano, maybe I could tear my Air magic away from the conglomerated cast and save the cat.

Sweat dripped off the tip of my nose. Tears mingled with it. The edges of my vision doubled, then all of it trebled. I felt a shock of cold from above and knew that Mr. Waban had finally begun his circle overhead. The fire didn't need our help, and I didn't have the power of speech anymore.

"Ian?"

I couldn't answer Charles, just jerked my chin up.

Nox cried out again, trying to wrangle the stream of water at the goon behind Tony. The magical pressure I'd been fighting eased as the others joined my trajectory and I could see again, but we turned it too late. Another explosion shook the old building just as the goon swung the knife down.

The two figures tumbled like the people on the Tarot card, The Tower. I thought about how Maddie had gotten that card on the first day I remembered meeting her and Nox. I should have known the portent had meaning, even if a Magus turned the card over instead of a Psychic.

The flames died. Over my shoulder came a series of howls and growls. One wolf pointed, and the bears dug. Nox and Charles and Olivia and Bianca held back, but I couldn't help myself. I had to see. Letting go of my boyfriend's hand, I jogged over to look.

They lay in a jumble of limbs, Tony sprawled face-down on top of the goon. The knife's hilt stuck out of his side under the ribs, but his chest rose and fell.

The goon's didn't. His eyes stared, unblinking. Reflected in his glassy eyes was the wheeling shadow of the ice dragon above, passing across the moon.

When the EME crew shouldered me aside, I watched them. One was an Air Magus like me, her wand creating a focused gust strong enough to lift Tony and turn him on his back. He saw me but soon looked past. I turned. He'd filled his gaze with Olivia's visage.

The owl shifter stopped struggling and blinked. She and Bianca let the crew hustle them into a second ambulance, separate from the one they'd put the two cat shifters in.

And just like that, they were all gone. It was over. My limbs felt leaden, my face like ice. Maybe that was from all the ice, I don't know. But when Charles rushed to my side and flung his arms around me, I thawed.

Our tears ran like rivers in flood, carrying us down the alley and back to the car we'd come in. Inside, on the way back to campus, my voice returned.

"Next time, I'm gonna make a difference." I leaned my head on his shoulder.

"What do you mean, Ian?" He ran his fingers over my curls.

"I mean, I know what major to declare now, Charles."

That was the night I decided to pursue a career as an Emergency Medical Magus.

NINE LIVES

The series continues with *Nine Lives,* coming soon to Amazon and Kindle Unlimited.

CONNECT WITH THE AUTHOR

Find D.R. Perry Online

Website: https://drperryauthor.com/

Author Central: http://www.amazon.com/-/e/B00O6851HO

Facebook: https://www.facebook.com/drpperry/

Mailing List: https://app.mailerlite.com/webforms/landing/
p9i8u6

Twitter: https://twitter.com/DRPerry22

ALSO BY D.R. PERRY

Providence Paranormal College

Bearly Awake (Book 1)

Fangs for the Memories (Book 2)

Of Wolf and Peace (Book 3)

Dragon My Heart Around (Book 4)

Djinn and Bear It (Book 5)

Roundtable Redcap (Book 6)

Better Off Undead (Book 7)

Ghost of a Chance (Book 8)

Nine Lives (Book 9)

Fan or Fan Knot (Book 10)

Hawthorn Academy

Familiar Strangers (Book 1)

Acting in Kindness (Book 2)

Fire of Justice (Book 3)

Gallows Hill Academy

Year One: Sorrow and Joy (Book one)

For other books by DR Perry please see her Amazon author page.

OTHER LMBPN PUBLISHING BOOKS

To be notified of new releases and special promotions from LMBPN publishing, please join our email list:

http://lmbpn.com/email/

For a complete list of books published by LMBPN please visit the following pages:

https://lmbpn.com/books-by-lmbpn-publishing/